Before the Fairytale
The Girl
With no Name

ISCAH

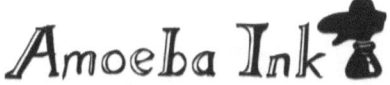
Amoeba Ink

Cover Art by Maxim Nossevitch

Copyright 2012-2013 Iscah
All Rights Reserved
Published by Amoeba Ink co.

www.amoebaink.com

ISBN 978-0-9835519-5-9
epub ISBN 978-0-9835519-2-8

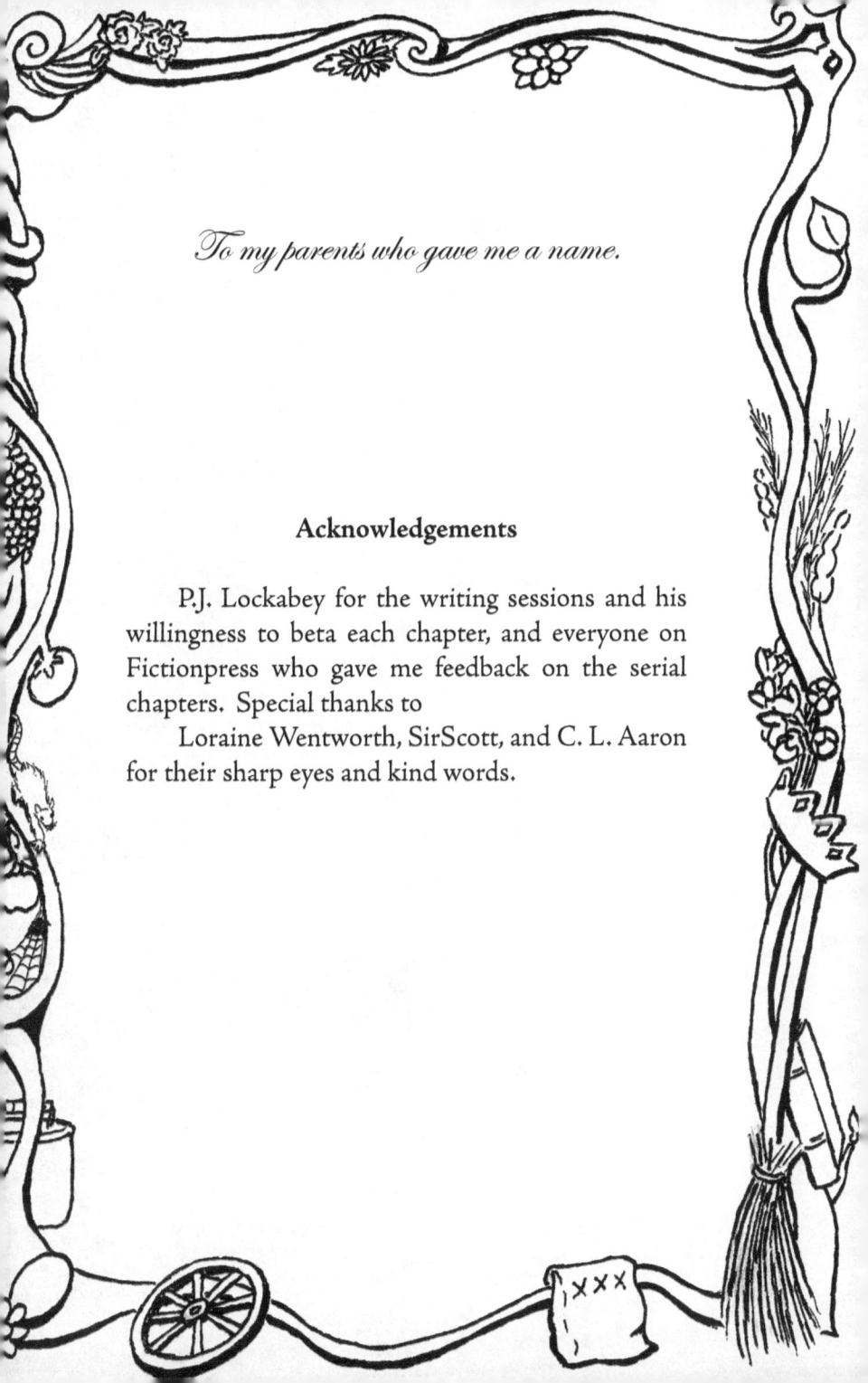

To my parents who gave me a name.

Acknowledgements

P.J. Lockabey for the writing sessions and his willingness to beta each chapter, and everyone on Fictionpress who gave me feedback on the serial chapters. Special thanks to
Loraine Wentworth, SirScott, and C. L. Aaron for their sharp eyes and kind words.

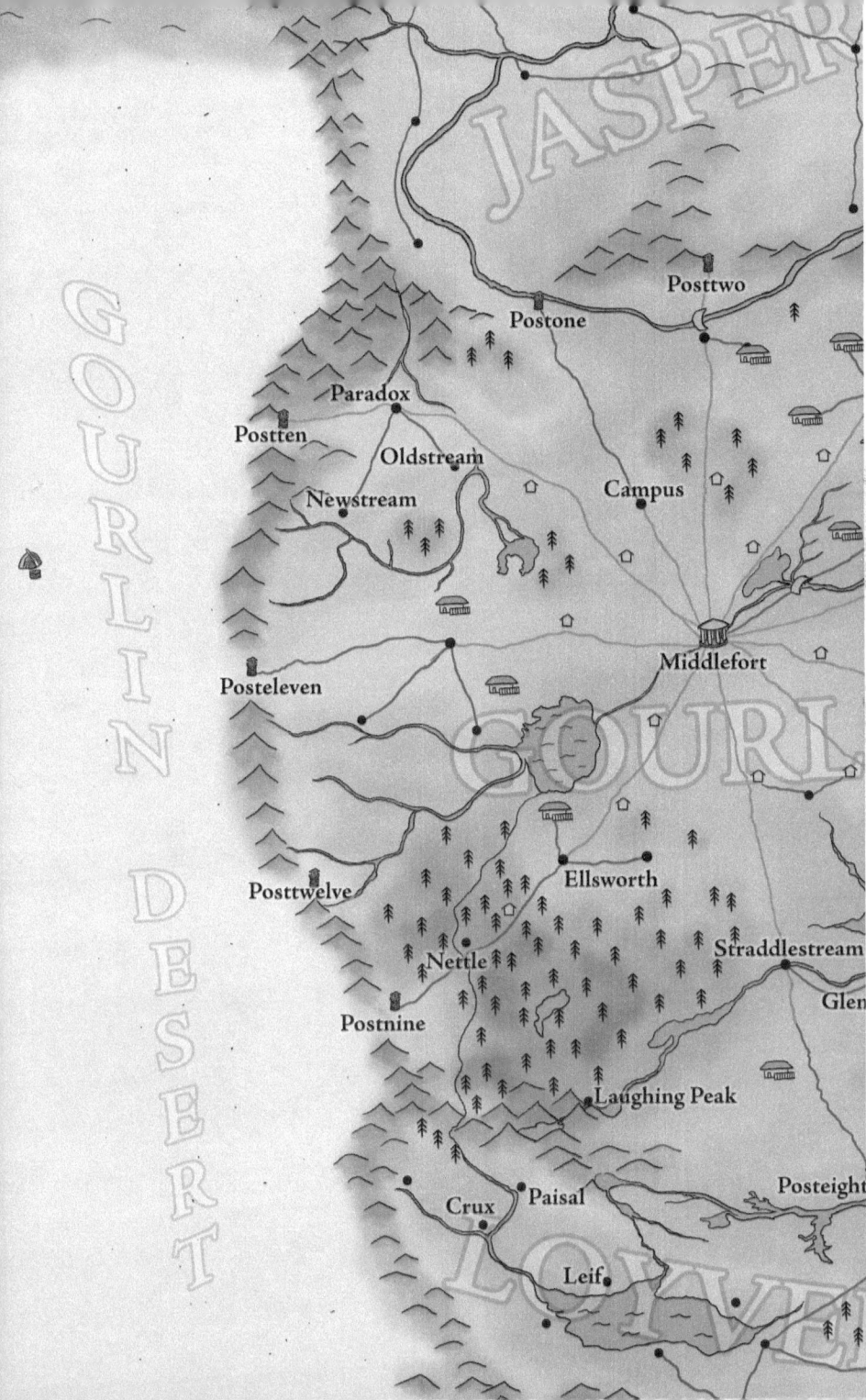

Prologue

O nce upon a time there was a girl with no name. She lived in the landlocked country of Gourlin in a small cabin with a very old man who was her keeper and only friend. She was not unloved nor very lonely for the whole of the world sang to her, but she had her share of difficulties.

It was not uncommon in this time for women to die in childbirth, and this was the fate that claimed her mother. Her mother had every intention of naming her, but she had waited for two things that never happened. She had waited to look in her child's eyes, and she had waited for her husband to return from his journey. But through the long months her child grew inside her, she sang to her daughter every day and told her secrets and stories that were still buried in the girl's soul.

The first person to look in the child's eyes other than the midwife was the elderly man who was to keep her. He thought it proper that she be named by one of her parents, so he also waited for her father to return. In the meantime, he called her Little and that worked well enough.

The girl's father had every intention of returning. He had left his most precious possessions in the care of his new wife and their elderly friend and taken only the bare essentials for his journey. Like many in Gourlin, he had heard the story of how their western desert had more than doubled in size overnight. Unlike many in Gourlin, he had a guess as to why. Perhaps if he had known he had a daughter coming, he may not have gone at all, but it is hard to say. No one plans to be murdered. No one expects the companion who had fought hard against wind and wave by their side for weeks on end in a small boat to reach a shore abandoned three centuries ago by their ancestors to show such treachery. But a black heart had been hidden behind an unassuming face and mild manner.

The one advantage of the girl's father never being aware of her was it kept her existence a perfect secret from the black hearted man as well.

Little and her keeper led a quiet life. Her parents had left her no great wealth in gold but a healthy stack of twenty or so books, many of them on magic, but two were handwritten journals about her father's travels. To the girl, they were a great treasure.

Chapter 1

The girl with no name had a peculiar talent and affliction. She could change her shape at will. While a potentially useful skill later in life, all she accomplished with it in her infancy was to frighten away her nursemaids. Babies offer enough challenges without suddenly turning into cats or cooking pots.

The old man did as best he could. He had no children of his own, but he had raised his share of dogs, cats, pigs, and chickens. While too old to be very fast, he was old enough to be patient. So when the crawling babe turned herself into a sack of flour and the last nursemaid quit from terror and frustration, he waited calmly for three days until she grew hungry or bored enough to turn back into a crying baby. When she became a cat, he poured her milk in a saucer. When she became a bird, he filled a dish with seed and allowed her to fly in and out the open window. When she became a snake, he shut her in a basket until she decided to be a baby again.

As she grew out of infancy and into childhood, she gained better control over her ability and spent most of her time as a girl. The old man bought her dresses, carved toys for her out of wood, and made her dolls from scraps and stuffing. He taught her to clean and cook, feed the chickens and collect the eggs. In the evenings, he read to her.

The old man had the talent and affliction of being rather wiser than most of his neighbors. Though he had been born with a name and made good use of it for most of his life, at this eve of his existence, the villagers referred to him simply as Elder.

When the first nursemaid returned to town talking of an evil shape-shifting infant that had killed its mother and clearly been sired by no human father, the people laughed at her. She was an old widow, though not nearly as old as the Elder, and was given to flights of fancy. The second nursemaid was a very young girl. When she returned telling stories about a baby that turned into a cat, they thought she was too easily influenced by the old widow. But the mayor's sister was a practical spinster without an ounce of fancy in her bones. So when she said the baby turned into a sack of flour, the stories of the other two gained new credence.

On the advice of his sister, the mayor and seven armed men went to visit the cottage of the old man on the outskirts of the village. They knocked on the door and explained their business. The old man listened politely as he could, but when they finished speaking, he began to chuckle.

"Why are you laughing, Elder?" they asked.

"Forgive me," he said. "But never before have I seen seven armed men frightened of a sleeping babe."

Embarrassed, one of the men said, "We're not afraid, Elder. We simply wish to see the child."

"Have you never seen one before?" asked the old man.

"Not one that changes into cats and cooking pots," said the mayor.

"But surely," said the old man. "You have seen a cat? And you have seen a cooking pot?"

"Well, certainly," huffed the mayor.

"Then I don't believe you will see anything you have not seen before," chuckled the old man.

"Surely it frightens you to live with such a creature!" exclaimed the mayor.

"You mean the child?"

"Yes, the child."

"Oh, no, I am old enough not to be frightened by children."

"No, no, Elder. It is not a normal child. My sister is reliable. We know the child changes."

"Well, I should hope so," said the old man. "A child that never changed would be a sad creature indeed. A mother may say she wishes to keep her babe small forever, but imagine if it never grew, never learned to speak or walk. It would be a great misfortune."

"You misunderstand me," the mayor said impatiently. "The widow saw the child change into a bird, and my sister saw it become a cooking pot and a sack of flour. Do you deny it?"

"I have no reason to."

"So you admit the child changes!"

"I believe we concluded all children do."

"But not into birds or cats or things that are not human!"

"No indeed, unless you count imagination," said the old man. "If she can do as you say, then I find myself the keeper of a rather unique child. But she is sleeping, so please keep your voice down."

The mayor scowled while the men shuffled their feet. In a quieter voice, he said, "It is my duty to guard the village and protect it from dangers." The old man nodded politely, and the mayor continued. "So you understand that I can not allow this child to stay in the village."

"I'm afraid I do not understand," said the old man, now

frowning. "I've never seen a child, a cat, or a pot, nor any combination of the three that was a danger to anyone, much less in need of seven armed men to escort it out of town."

"We can take the child by force, if we have to," said the mayor, though he could see his men would be extremely reluctant to do so.

"Oh, I'm sure you could," said the old man. "But I do not see how the child is a danger...unless as a cat she scratched someone?...no?....Well, perhaps as a bird she pecked the widow?...no?...Did she burn her nurse as a cooking pot? Or perhaps your sister finds bags disagreeable? Surely, I am far enough from the other houses that her crying troubles no one's sleep but my own?"

The men shook their heads. The mayor tried, but he could think of no argument. "Very well, Elder," he sighed. "We leave the child to your care."

The mayor and the men returned to their homes. The mayor's mind was not entirely easy about the changing child, but soon after, his sister ran off with a passing soldier. The reliability of the only reliable witness now in question, the girl and her guardian were left in peace.

The affliction of the wise was that they often forget that others do not share their wisdom. The old man believed that reason once seen would always remain clear, and so when the girl turned six, like any responsible adult with a child in Gourlin, he sent her to school to learn to read.

Chapter 2

U nlike its neighbors, the country of Gourlin had the very sensible policy of teaching its children to read. Every child between the ages of six and twelve was expected to attend school at the town hall for three hours, three days a week where they taught three subjects: their own language Western Coastal, basic math for commerce, and the language of their neighboring countries.

Paper was expensive, and books were rare among those who were not rich. Most children practiced their letters and numbers with mud and sticks on thin pieces of slate. So while few adults were great readers or mathematicians, they were still considered very useful skills. It gave the country of Gourlin a measure of educational pride and reason to feel superior to its neighbors.

The girl with no name became a great reader, but she only spent three weeks attending the village school before she decided she would learn better and more pleasantly under the tutelage of her elderly keeper. There was a very simple reason why the other children pelted her with their mud and sticks and cruel words. It was the same thing that had driven her ancestors from the land three centuries ago.

Fear.

The first day of school the teacher asked the girl her name, and she could give him no answer. The children laughed. After some frustration and a few more questions,

7

the teacher settled on calling her No Name.

Children are well known for their ability to turn any name into a taunt, and No Name was ripe for taunting. This was not fear, simply childishness. The children's fear grew because, while the girl had better control over her ability, it was not quite perfect. Several times, while looking at the eyes of another student, hers would become the same color. Her hair might grow curlier or straighter or start shifting hue depending on what she was thinking about.

The children were at first startled and curious about the talent. They asked their parents about it, and while one might hope parents would be less childish than their children, this did not prove true. Their parents made wild speculations and mixed details, which only turned the children's curiosity and concern to fear and disgust. By the third week, they were throwing their mud and sticks at the girl.

The mud washed off and bruises from the small sticks healed, but it is much harder to get rid of words. The cruelest of these was how the children had mixed up the mother with the nursemaid and told the girl her mother had run off from fear of her. Being a stranger to lies, it never occurred to the small girl to question what they had said, and it weighed in her heart.

The old man could have set the story right, but the child never asked. He wiped her tears and washed off the mud and offered to teach her at home.

Chapter 3

They lived a quiet and happy life for a time. The girl grew taller, and the old man grew older. She read her father's books and learned that far away and across the sea there were other people like her. People who could hear the world sing and make magic and even some who could change their shape. They were called shifters, and it was very comforting to know that though her talent was rare even in the land of wizards she was not the only one. Her talent was a product of magic but did not make her a danger.

The books revealed to her that the essence of magic was to change a pattern. To control the effect, a magic user must first understand the pattern. Anyone could change a pattern, people did it constantly, but the art of magic was akin to the art of an instrument. Anyone can pluck a string, but it takes talent and study to have the strings produce a song. As with music, some were born with a certain talent and ear for the patterns of the world. For them the wind did not merely blow, it sang. A flower did not simply grow, it composed. Those with the greatest talent could change the composition.

Most magic is subtle, so it was easy enough to keep secret. They had few visitors, so there was no one to notice that a song helped more easily light the fire or that the flavor of the wood in the walls had been changed to keep away mice and bugs.

Still the girl knew that people were afraid of her. The books only made the vaguest mention of why the wizards had left the land and crossed the sea, something about kings and sages and counsels, but the girl suspected it had more to do with them not liking to see sticks and mud and cruel words thrown at their children.

But she also learned from the old man that someone without magic and someone with it could live together in perfect harmony. Three hundred years ago, which in some ways was a very long time and in other ways not long at all, the wizards had lived in Gourlin and the surrounding lands, so her ancestral home was also the one where she lived. She wondered if those wizards had left anything behind.

She asked the old man if he thought there might be. He told her there were some people who still called themselves magicians in the land, but most people did not believe in magic anymore. "It is hard to believe in what you can not see."

So the girl gathered eggs from their six chickens, milked their two goats, read her books, and listened to the world sing.

And then one morning after she had gathered the eggs and made a breakfast, she went to wake the old man, but he would not wake. He looked peaceful but cold, and she ran to the village center to find help. The men came, and the old man was buried.

The next morning the mayor came to tell the girl that she must leave. The old man had no children or wife of his own, and the law was clear. His property now belonged to the village. She could no longer live there.

The girl's heart was heavy as she packed her clothes and books and what little money she could find. She took the

10

cooking pots and wooden bowls and hitched the goats to the old man's small wagon. Then she set off to find her father.

Chapter 4

Step by step the girl with no name walked down the dirt road that led away from the village. She did not know where the road led, only that people came and left this way so the road must go to somewhere. The nearly full moon shone down on them, singing its quiet song that changed everyday but was always the same as the month before. The stars chorused along like the chirping of crickets. The trees alongside the path hummed in their sleep. It was both sad and comforting to know that the night had not noticed the passing of her only friend. It was as it always was and would be.

She let her goats set the pace since they had the greater burden. She was in no hurry. The only plan she could form was to follow the road and see where it led. When she grew tired, she took her goats off the road and tied them to a tree. She rolled the small wagon just out of their reach, for goats will eat most anything they can reach, and took an old quilt from it. The wagon tilted back on the axle of its two wheels, and she spread her blanket under the meager shelter it provided and slept.

She woke a few hours later to the scream of the goats. A lone wolf was drawing ever closer, panting in anticipation as its helpless prey tugged against their ropes. There was no one around and no time or need for modesty. The girl slipped out of her dress and changed into a bear. She charged towards the predator, roaring out all the anger she felt. She took a swipe with her claws, but the wolf darted away into the underbrush. She was in no mood to chase after it.

The goats, not quite bright enough to understand they had been rescued, began to work themselves up into an even greater panic. The girl returned to her dress, became a girl again, and tried to reassure them. At first, she did not approach them. She sat still and sang a song of comfort, for most magic is subtle. After a time, the goats grew calm. The girl approached and stroked their necks until they had forgiven her. Then she milked the she-goats and made a breakfast of milk and berries.

After breakfast, they continued down the road until they found a stream. The girl realized she was ill prepared for travel. They drank their fill, but the girl had nothing well designed to carry water. She had nothing to shelter them at night from foe or storm. In her haste to leave, she had brought very little food. The goats were content to eat the plants on the roadside and nibbled happily on anything that had managed to set root on their path, but the girl's stomach was more selective. The goats were good for milk but could not provide bread, meat, or vegetables.

The girl put a little water in one of the pots but was anxious for her books and dare not fill it lest it spill over. She urged the goats to keep a steady pace, hoping they would reach a town or inn soon.

Around noon they passed a soldier riding a tall, brown unicorn with a copper horn. "Sir, do you have any food I could buy?" she asked.

"I offer my apology, little vagabond," he said. "But I only carry enough to take me to the next town."

"How far this way until I can buy food?" she asked.

"Best go home, little runaway."

13

"I have no home," she said.

"No father or mother?"

"I'm looking for my father," the girl said. "His name is Mortagin." She knew this from his journals. "Do you know him?"

The soldier shook his head. "Your mother sent you?"

"My mother left me long ago," the girl said.

"I must wonder then where you got the goats."

"They belonged to the Elder I lived with, but he died, and the mayor said his property belongs to the village."

"So it does," said the soldier with a frown. "Including the goats. Unless he specifically made a gift of them before he died?"

"Not specifically," said the girl, a little perplexed.

"Then you are a little thief," said the soldier. "I must take you back to the village with me to return the goats and determine your punishment."

Other girls may have cried as the soldier dismounted and stepped closer, looking very formidable and official with his sword and armor, but the girl with no name was too angry to cry. She had lost her home to the village which had shown her no pity. Since they were unsuitable to travel, she had been forced to abandon her chickens, but to have her goats taken as well was unbearable. If they wanted her goats, what would stop them from claiming the wagon or small amount of gold and silver in her pocket?

As the soldier reached out his arm for her, she let her eyes grow black and began to growl like a bear. He jumped back with a startled exclamation. The girl tried to give form to her anger. She let her fingers grow into claws, her skin to grow dark and thorny.

The soldier forgot his sword, ran back to his unicorn,

and galloped away as fast the unicorn's hooves could fly. Before he was completely out of sight, the girl was a girl again. She was still angry but much less scared. She had learned fear could be useful.

Chapter 5

The girl with no name had no interest in terrifying the countryside. She had read enough stories with ferocious dragons greedily guarding treasures and terrorizing villages to know such creatures were always slain in the end. She was old enough to start imagining about being wooed by a heroic figure and would prefer to be the rescued damsel or clever maid who outwitted the beast.

Knowing she had a way to protect herself did allow her to continue down the road with more confidence. Her stomach was a growing, growling concern, but to her delight a few more hours walk brought her in sight of a tavern. The pleasant smell of baking bread and simmering stew stretched out to greet her and carried her the last quarter mile to the tavern door. She exchanged a piece of silver for a full belly, a room for the night, and a stall for the goats.

The tavern keepers had a few young sons and a daughter close to the girl's own age. They were too far from town to attend school regularly, so they also took their lessons at home. The daughter was intrigued to see a girl traveling by herself and took to sweeping around her feet as an excuse to ask her questions. The girl was careful to edit her story, so she spoke of the search for her father but did not mention the death of the Elder.

The tavern children were too short on friends to poke fun at potential playmates. They thought her lack of a name made the girl an intriguing and mysterious figure. When she saw their curiosity and kindness, the girl decided to share her books with them. Aside from his journals and a few books on magic, her father had collected a small library of histories and fables during his travels. The girl read to the tavern children from an adventure book with fairies and dragons and other things people no longer believed. Their parents were so delighted that they gave her an extra night at no charge and may have welcomed her for several more, but the girl had not forgotten her own quest. After the second night and second breakfast at the tavern, she bid her new friends goodbye, and they wished each other happiness before she parted.

She had learned of a town called Ellsworth, about a day's travel away, from the tavern keeper, who bought the morning goats' milk from her and packed a lunch for her journey. With a much lighter step, she walked down the long road with a song on her lips and happier goats.

Chapter 6

Before nightfall, she reached the town. It was a larger town than the one she had left. It had a proper town square with stone-paved streets, and two-story buildings with apartments over shops. She enjoyed the sound of the goats' hooves on the stone.

"Hey, girl!" a man with full brown beard and full round face barked at her. "No animals in the town square."

The girl bit back her frustration, wishing rules and laws were posted more plainly. "Sorry, sir, I'm new here. Is there an inn where I can take my goats?"

The man had a barking voice, but her politeness took some of the bite from it. "Back down where you came, take the dirt path, right or left makes no matter. Come to the stone road on the opposite side of the square, and the inn is a little ways down the stone road."

"Thank you, sir," the girl said. Before she could turn her goats around, the loud clopping of hooves drew her attention to a horse-drawn carriage making good speed through the town square. The street was wide enough there was not any danger, but the girl pulled her goats closer to the edge to be sure.

She waited for the man to bark at the carriage driver as he had at her, but the man merely bowed his head and waited for the carriage to pass.

"Are horses not considered animals?" the girl asked after the carriage had passed them.

The bearded man looked at her askew. "You can not expect noblemen to follow the rules of commoners."

"Why not?" the girl asked, but the bearded man only laughed in answer.

The girl turned her goats around and headed for the dirt road. It was far more traveled than the long road she had walked before, littered with ruts, animal droppings, and an unhealthy smell. She tried to be careful where she stepped. She could understand why they wouldn't want animals soiling the pretty stone streets, but she also thought they might be far easier to clean.

The dirt road was a longer way around than the stone streets at the town center, but she reached the stone road and the inn before the sunset. It was twice as large as the tavern she had last stayed in, and there were a lot more people walking about.

She tied her goats to a post outside and hurried in to inquire about a room and a stable. A woman stood at a desk in the entry hall. "May I have a room please?" the girl asked.

"I doubt you can pay for a room, dear, or are there more in your party?"

"I'm alone," the girl said. "Except for my goats."

"We don't allow goats in the room," the woman said with her brow cocked in a way that made the girl think she might be teasing.

"Of course not," she said. "I was hoping you had a stable. I have two goats and a small cart."

"Aye, we have a stable," the woman said. "My rooms are full, but I have a bed in the women's dorm. Half a silver each per night."

The girl handed the woman a silver and wrote her name

on the register, another thing that was new from the last inn. The woman handed her two wooden tokens with numbers burned into them and told her to present one at the stable.

The girl hurried back outside, breathed a sigh of relief to find her cart as she had left it, and took cart and goats around to the back. She paid a little extra money to have the goats fed and a little more extra to buy a dinner for herself.

While she ate her dinner, she asked a young man, who from overheard snippets she understood to be native to the town, "Do you know where I could learn all the laws of the town? Is there a place where they're all written down together?"

The young man laughed to hear a girl ask such a question. "I suppose you might find such a thing in the town hall."

"Aye," said his neighbor. "Or the bookstore. I think they have some law books there, though they don't take kindly to those who finger."

The girl felt her heart flutter. "A shop just for books?" she asked eagerly.

The men laughed again, but the girl was too happy to mind. She was growing more intrigued by the town and had nearly made up her mind to stay a few days rather than pass straight through.

After dinner, she was pointed up to the third floor and the women's dorm. It was a long room with two rows of bunk beds, packed close together with only a narrow pass between. She had never seen beds stacked on top of each other before. There were several women laying claim to a bed, some already asleep, others changing from day clothes to night clothes in front of all the other women. The girl had never shared a room before and found this all very strange.

She left her day clothes on, and after several minutes internal debate, climbed onto one of the top bunks, figuring if the thing fell through it was better to be on top than on bottom. The bed held, but now she spent a few minutes worrying what would happen if she rolled off in the night.

She might have spent all night worrying, but she had walked a long way that day. Before she could decide to try a bottom bed, she was fast asleep.

Chapter 7

The girl survived the night but nearly fell off the bed in the morning when she forgot her height. The sunlight poured through the window shutters, which had been flung open by some early riser, and the girl remembered the intriguing town that awaited her.

She went to give her goats their morning milking and tried to sell the extra to the innkeeper, but they were not interested. She drank what she could and offered the rest to the stablehands, who were glad to receive it.

After she finished attending the animals, the girl set out to explore the town square and find the bookshop. Having grown up in seclusion she had never seen a shop before, but she understood the word from stories the old man had told. She bought a bun from the baker's and asked him if he had ever known a man named Mortagin. He had not. Nor had the clerk in the candle shop nor the lady in the fabric store.

The dairy agreed to buy her goats' milk if she would bring it around back the next morning, but only at a tenth of the price they sold it. Still the girl thought it better than letting the milk go to waste. She bought an ounce of cheese from them.

She stopped to listen to an argument between a butcher and a farmer over the price of a cow. When the men parted, the girl asked the butcher. "Why were you arguing?"

"Not an argument, girl," the butcher corrected. "A negotiation. Men may talk in tones too rough for the ears of women folk, hey?"

"My ears are fine," the girl said, though she still did not understand the need to shout.

"What are you buying?" the butcher pressed.

"Nothing today. I'm staying at the inn and have no fire of my own."

The butcher snorted. The girl watched him for a while as he cleaned and sharpened his knives. A neatly dressed woman walked in with a basket under her arm, and the butcher smiled at her.

"Good morning, Adele," he said in a pleasant and gentle voice. "What will you have today?"

"A pound of beef," the woman said briskly, giving him a cool smile. The butcher chopped away merrily, wrapped the steak in a long, dry leaf and traded it for coin.

The woman tucked the meat into her basket and turned to find the girl staring at her. "Why do you stare?" the woman asked her just as briskly as she had ordered from the butcher.

"I was thinking how Adele is a very pretty name," the girl said.

The brisk woman suddenly smiled. Her cool face warmed. "Why thank you very much," she said and walked out the store. The girl stayed where she was, looking very thoughtful.

The butcher sighed. "Do you plan to stand there all day and pester my customers?"

"Oh, no, sorry," the girl said. "I was just thinking how funny it was that people can change so quickly." The butcher squinted one eye in response, and the girl left so she would not pester him any longer.

The town hall was easy to find, being quite literally the

center of the town. The first floor was devoted to meeting rooms. The girl walked up a curving stair to the second floor and through an open door, where a wrinkly old man sat behind a large desk. "Sir," she asked. "Is this where all the rules of the town are kept?"

"All the laws of the kingdom are here," he said. "What is it you want to know?"

"I was hoping to read all the town rules," she said.

The old man gained even more wrinkles as his white brows drew together. "All of them?"

"Yes, please."

"Those are all the laws of the town," the man said, pointing to a long wall full of books and scrolls. "And those," he said, pointing to the other rows of shelves. "Are rulings on how to interpret them."

The girl's mouth fell open. "How could anyone ever read all those?"

"I don't know if anyone has," the old man said. "Though I'm certainly familiar with most of them. Did you have a question?"

The girl looked at all the rule books, and while she had a great love of reading, even she was put off by it. "Don't you think it's rather silly to have so many rules that no one could ever read them all?"

The old man snorted irritably. "Nonsense, it's law. You can't expect the law to be simple."

"Then how do you expect anyone to follow it?" the girl asked.

"Common sense," the old man snapped. "Now ask a question or go about your business. I have no time for idle schoolchildren."

"Why do you need so many shelves for interpretations?"

the girl asked, too surprised to be daunted. "Are the laws so hard to understand?"

"Circumstances must be taken into account," the old man said.

"Like the horses of noblemen not being considered animals in the town square?"

"Precisely," the old man said. "You must make allowances for men's circumstances."

"I still think it sounds very silly," said the girl.

Chapter 8

When the girl stepped outside, she spotted a unicorn tied just beyond the stone-paved town square. This one had grey patches and a silver horn. Curious, she drew closer. The unicorn lowered its head and made it easy for her to stroke its forehead beneath the horn. "Are you an animal?" she asked.

The unicorn blinked at her as though to reproach, *no more than you are.* She stroked the unicorn's neck, feeling its strength and warmth, and heard a hum of happiness come from the animal. They parted ways, never to meet again, but for a minute or so they were very good friends.

She had almost finished her circuit of the square when she found the bookstore between the wine seller and the barrister. It was a small, narrow shop. A tall, narrow man stood behind the counter. "Do you need a binding?" he asked before looking at her.

"I don't think so," the girl said.

The bookseller glanced up at her. Keen eyes narrowed and inspected her fingers, dress, and boots for signs of dirt. "This is not a shop for idlers," he said. His voice was cautious as though he had yet to make up his mind about her. "Do you need something copied?"

"I was told this was a bookshop," the girl said.

The narrow man gave her a narrow smile. "You can see the books there, can't you?"

"Oh, yes," the girl said, smiling with the eagerness of youth and eyes alight as only a great reader who has found their first bookstore can light. One wall of the shop was lined with two sets of shelves. The shelves held books, neatly displayed like works of art.

"That shelf is new books, and the other is used ones, many of which we have restored," the bookseller told her. "Are you looking for something in particular?"

"My father," the girl said, while she squatted down to look at the oldest and dustiest books.

"Ah," the man said, as though this explained things. "He was to meet you here."

"That would be nice," the girl said. "But I don't think he's expecting me."

"He's a book lover then, and you hope to find him here?" the bookseller tried again.

"That's closer to it," the girl said. She carefully pulled the dustiest volume off the lowest shelf and gently blew the dust away. Out of habit, she asked, "Do you know a man named Mortagin?"

"I remember a man by that name," the bookseller said with a new note in his voice.

Surprised, the girl turned around quickly, the previously dusty volume cradled in her arms. "Does he live here in Ellsworth?"

The bookseller shook his head. "It was many year ago, but I remember a man named Mortagin. He had a short stiff beard and pretty young wife. Quite a traveler, but not a merchant, which is unusual and why I remember him."

"About twelve years ago?" the girl asked.

"There about," said the bookseller. "He bought a book on history and another on fairytales."

27

"I know the books," the girl said fondly. "Do you know where he went?"

"He had come from Middlefort and was heading away, made some talk of going to Tivin next, but if he went, I can not say."

The girl's heart sank. Tivin was another country, on the far side and south of the Gourlin desert. "Surely, you've seen him more recently than I have," said the bookseller, noticing her dejection.

"I've never seen him," the girl confessed.

"That is a sad story," said the bookseller. "Your mother left no clue for you?"

The girl shook her head. "But my father did leave me some books and his journals."

The bookseller's eyes lighted as only a bookseller's can do when books are scarce and he learns of new ones. "Bring them here around sunset, and I will help you search them for clues."

The girl was so happy that strands the color of gold shot through her hair. The bookseller saw this, but he said nothing.

Chapter 9

The girl with no name left the dusty volume at the bookseller's and danced her way back to the stable where she had left her goats and her books. She spent the afternoon poring over them. The journals did not tell a clear story. They were a jumble of sketches and notes that spoke of travels and broad interests but lacked personality, save in a few pages where her father had taken the time to write out a proper entry.

The first such entry read thus:

> The sea crossing was rough. We were tempted by the tempest surrounding the Floating Isle, but it proved too much for us. Our small boat was tossed about like a toy on the waves. Only the greatest determination and concentration allowed us to find a safe path through the rolling waters. We lost all bearings for a time. The night remained too cloudy to follow the stars, so we had only our peeks of the sun to guide us. I had faith that if we could stay on a western course we could make landfall before our rations ran out. In truth we would have died without Sargon's invaluable talent for enchanting the salt out of the water to make it drinkable. He was chosen for that skill, and I celebrate now the wisdom of that choice.
>
> We made landfall on the country of Cordance, by chance in a deserted portion of the beach. After making a few repairs to the boat, we sailed north, keeping in close sight of the shore and discovered a large number of scattered settlements and

lonely fishermen until at last encountering a large port such as I have only seen on rivers in our Wizard's Land. There is clearly no guardian patrolling this shore.

I had worried that three hundred years of separation would leave the language unintelligible, but other than some peculiarities in phrasing, accent, and idioms, we were able to get along fairly well. Seaside sees it's share of traders from northern and southern shores, so our foreign fumbles did not draw undue attention.

This was followed by a list of idioms and common phrases in the Cordance variation on Western Coastal. Some of which were very familiar to the girl in Gourlin, but others amusingly peculiar to Cordance.

She turned the pages past a crude map of Cordance until she reached another entry.

In Pinnacle City, Sargon and I agreed to part ways. He will travel the coastal countries, while I go east and further inland. Our plan is to meet back here in three years time to compare notes, and if the king wills, return home.

And so followed more crude maps and curious lists. Her father had journeyed around north of the Gourlin desert by joining a caravan. He had traveled the countries that bordered Gourlin to the north and east, all the way to the Eastern Road, which promised more to explore than three years would allow. He then traveled south, nearly to another sea. His motives were unclear, but he double back to a mountain settlement and there met the young woman who would become the girl's mother.

I find as I travel a willful ignorance of magic. Its presence has been assigned to children's stories and charlatans. These tricksters have led the general populace to believe that magic is purely a product of their ancestor's imagination and ignorance. I do nothing to dissuade this belief in a general way, but the loneliness of my journey does incite in me a desire for kindred spirits.

Having found a young woman whose laughter lifts my spirits and contains a desire for exploration as strong as my own, I found myself compelled to marry her. I will make my reports as I am duty bound to do but wonder if my companion would be capable of making his voyage back to our land without my assistance.

The girl noticed that the sky was beginning to dim and hurried back to the bookstore with the books under her arm. The keen-eyed bookseller was closing up shop when she arrived.

"Come into the backroom," he said as he barred the shutters.

The girl followed him and found the backroom larger than the front. "We do most of our work, the copying and binding back here," he explained. There were several tables and benches in the backroom, many of them spread with open projects. There were shelves here too, but rather than books, they were lined with stacks of paper, leather and cloth, as well as ink bottles, quills, brushes, and other tools of bookmakers.

"I do most of the binding work myself," he continued, "but I employ a couple of scribes. Most of our orders are to copy short documents for legal affairs, but between those demands, I keep them busy making books."

"I think I would like that kind of work," the girl said.

The bookseller looked dubious. "It's tedious, precise, and exacting work, not suited to the temperament of young girls."

"I'll get older," the girl said. "But for now, I'd like to find my father first."

"Naturally," the bookseller said. He lit a candle and motioned for her to lay the books before him. "Do you have a place to stay, Mortagin's daughter? I'm sorry I haven't asked your name yet."

"You can call me Mortagin's daughter," said the girl. "I need to find my father to learn my name."

"Is that a peculiar practice of wizards to leave their children without naming them?" the bookseller asked shrewdly.

"I have no idea," the girl said. "Perhaps I can ask when I find him."

"Your father was looking for books that held lingering traces of wizards from the time before they departed our land. After a long talk, he agreed to show me a little magic," said the bookseller. "Do you know any magic, Mortagin's daughter?"

"I've learned a little from books," admitted the innocent.

"Would you show me?"

The girl had never been asked for a demonstration before and was quiet for a moment pondering how she might please the bookseller, for most magic is subtle and not given to show. As night was falling, she hummed and worked her fingers around the candle flame, brightening its glow.

"I can change the taste of wood to repel bugs," the girl said.

The bookseller smiled. "If you could do that for my shelves and books, it would be very useful."

"I'd be happy to," the girl said eagerly.

The bookseller shook his head. "You should always ask for payment for your services, child. Otherwise men will take advantage of you."

"Oh," said the girl, seeing sense in this advice. "What would you pay me to keep the bugs from your shelves then?"

"Where are you sleeping, little magician?" asked the bookseller.

"At the inn, but there are lots of other people in the same room."

"I have a wife and two young children, so I can't take you home," said the bookseller. "But if you don't mind a pallet in the shop, you may sleep here. I have done so myself when an order must be filled quickly."

"I do think I'd like that better," agreed the girl.

The shopkeeper smiled. "I must trust you're not a thief, but I think a chance to look through your books will compensate me for the risk."

"You said you would help me find clues," the girl reminded him.

"And I will," the bookseller said. "We will make that part of our bargain." He carefully turned the pages of the journal with his long fingers.

"I tried to start at the beginning," said the girl.

"Normally a good place to start," said the bookseller. "But I think we are more interested in the end." With that he took the second journal and found the last page with any writing on it. "Here are the last words in your father's journal: Flying caravan may be fastest."

The girl looked at the words and frowned. "What does it mean?"

The bookseller opened his mouth and closed it again. "Perhaps we had best answer that in the morning when our minds are fresh and the sun will save us the cost of a candle."

The girl pouted with disappointment but thought it best not to argue. Before the night grew too dark, he walked back with her to retrieve the rest of her books and belongings, at least the ones that were not easily replaced. The goats and the wagon would spend another night at the inn stable.

As they returned, the bookseller explained that he lived above the shop, so he did not have far to travel and would hear any trouble downstairs. While she knew it was a warning for her against mischief, it also made her feel safe and easy as she prepared her pallet that night.

The stars hummed a lullaby, and a family of termites nibbled to a dull tempo on the floorboards. "You must find a new home tomorrow," the girl whispered to them.

There were limits to how small she could make herself. She had tried to be an insect once, and while she managed the basic form, she could only shrink to the size of a small dog. There were spells to make things shrink very small, but they were not for living things. Living things were too complex and rarely survived being squished together. The largest thing she had ever been able to change into was that medium sized bear.

But dreams lack all restrictions. So that night she could be small as a bug or big as a mountain.

Chapter 10

The next morning the girl used magic to change the taste of all the wood in the shop to repel termites and other bugs while the bookseller read her father's journals between customers. "Did you find anymore about the flying caravan?" the girl asked at lunchtime.

"Not yet," said the bookseller. "But I haven't finished reading them yet."

A week passed while the bookseller read the first journal. He was kind enough and gave the girl a few jobs to keep her busy while she waited for him to finish.

The bookseller's wife was more uncertain of their new tenant. "My husband tells me you're looking for your father?" she asked, when she brought down lunch for them. The girl nodded, and the wife frowned. "You have eyes like my husband," she said shrewdly.

"Oh, I'm sorry," said the girl, for she had been copying unintentionally again. She closed her eyes and rubbed them while she concentrated. "Is that better?"

The wife said nothing but walked away quickly.

The girl offered to read books to the children like she had before, but the bookseller said that was his wife's job. She was their teacher outside of school and liked this work. His wife kept the children away from her, so that the girl only saw them when they left for school in the mornings.

She tried to get the scribes to teach her their trade, but

they insisted the work was not suited to young girls. She milked her goats in the morning and found a place to sell the milk, which paid for their keeping at night, and when she had no jobs to do, she read.

Another week passed before the bookseller finished reading the second journal.

"Did you learn more about the caravan?" the girl asked, and again the bookseller shook his head.

"I did learn more about your father," he said. "While I do not mean to discourage you, I think he would have returned if he were able."

"What do you think has kept him?" asked the girl.

"He may have been forced to return by his companion and king to the land of wizards," said the bookseller. "He may have fallen ill. He may be lost. He may have been imprisoned. I can not tell you why he stayed away. Only that you can get a sense of a writer from his writing, and this is not a man who would abandon his child."

The girl with no name blinked back the tears that formed in her eyes. She could not remember being so happy and so sad at the same time. "If he can't come to me, then I'll go to him," she said with determination.

"Then I can tell you this," said the bookseller. "The flying caravan travels from Laughing Peak to the town of Paradox to Moore's High in Uritz."

"You already knew?" the girl realized. "You could have told me that two weeks ago!"

"And watch you run off before I was sure I had not missed something more likely," said the bookseller.

The girl still felt angry but could not find words for it.

"You could go south to Laughing Peak. It's a little closer, but there's no good road leading directly to it. Or you can

follow the stone road to Middlefort and then take another to Paradox."

The girl nodded, and without another word, she left to get her goats.

Chapter 11

The country of Gourlin was very proud of its roads. There were ten stone roads leading out from Middlefort, as straight as roads could reasonably be, to the ten largest towns and from the ten towns there were other roads, not always stone, leading to the small villages and outposts.

As the girl walked down the even road with her goats and wagon, she found herself changing with each step. One moment she was angry with the bookseller for delaying her journey, and with the next step, she was sorry she left so quickly. There were a few times she almost went back for proper goodbyes, but somewhere farther down this road, she might have a father, a father who might be trapped in a prison or lying sick in a bed, who might need a rescue, and who might have a name for her. These thoughts kept her traveling forward.

The road was not busy in the same way the town square had been busy, but the girl passed more people in larger groups coming up and down it. Some gave her a wave, a nod, or a smile as they went by, and others paid her no mind. Sometimes there were minutes between meetings; other times there were hours.

Watching the other travelers did make her wish she had a cart big enough to ride. Her feet were sore from walking. She began to think eventually she would want to buy new shoes, and she would need to pay for a night in a tavern.

Her mind worked as hard as her feet as she walked down the long, nearly-straight stone road.

It was after dark when she reached the tavern. She was relieved to discover she still had enough to pay for a room and a meal, but the lightness of her purse concerned her. The snippets of conversation she heard from other travelers troubled her. Many of them remarked how things cost more or sold for more in Middlefort.

The girl listed in her mind the things she had brought with her, but there were few of them she was willing to part with.

"I don't like being poor," she said out loud, realizing for the first time that she knew the name for this condition.

"No one does, little urchin," said an older woman further down the table.

"I would try to find work," she told the woman. "But I need to travel to Paradox first to find my father."

"Find work with a caravan then," the woman suggested.

"I'll try that," the girl said, feeling her spirits brighten a little. After all a tavern seemed like a good place to find travelers, and all of them seemed to be going to or coming from Middlefort.

It took asking nearly everyone in the tavern, some of them twice, but the girl finally found someone who agreed to let her travel with them in return for doing the wash. They left early the next morning, a small group of merchants, and when they stopped for lunch not far from a stream, the girl was given a basket of clothes and told to hurry.

There was no time to let everything dry. The party had two wagons with wooden roofs. The girl had to clamber up the side with a stepladder and tie the wash to the roof, so the sun would dry away what she had been unable to wring out. After the rest of the party was refreshed, and she was very tired, they set off again. She saved a few steps by finding an easy perch on the tailboard of the larger wagon, but every bump threatened to throw her off.

She thought the journey might be easier if she turned into a bird, but she did not think she could keep control of her goats or carry all her books that way. It would mean leaving too much behind.

They reached another tavern before nightfall, where she enjoyed a good night's sleep, and the next morning they repeated the same process, though this time her water had to be drawn from a well.

She should have been more tired, but new sights kept her alert. After the second tavern, the traffic on the road became heavier, and the sight of houses grew more frequent. By the time they passed the well, the road was lined with clusters of shops, even though they had not yet reached the city walls. She could see them in the distance. While most of the country gradually sloped inwards to this central city, Middlefort itself was up on a hill. Not a high hill or a sharp hill, but high enough. She could see a little over the walls. The city seemed to ripple in the distance and spill over into the surrounding countryside.

To one who could hear the stars chirp and the sun sing, it buzzed. All the people in the city made it buzz, while the stones whispered ancient stories. There were plenty of horses on this portion of the stone road, even a few unicorns. The merchants stopped at one of the shops, and the girl rested her feet. While she sat, she saw her first pegasus. Its wings looked too small to let it fly, but she still found it a striking sight.

For her day's work, the merchants covered another night's stay for her at an inn just outside the city. In the morning, she thanked them, and they parted ways. The merchants were not traveling any farther north.

She milked her goats, drank a little, and managed to trade the rest for some breakfast. While she ate, she tried to plan the rest of her route. There was a road that circled around the city, and therefore no need for her to actually travel inside the walls. While it might be a little longer, it would be a simpler and less crowded route.

In truth, the girl found a place where the buildings had sprouted like trees (some just as tall) to be a little intimidating. She decided to skirt the city. Even walking around rather than through, she saw more shops and houses than she had ever imagined.

The people seemed endless. Even in Ellsworth, she believed with enough time she could have come to know everyone at least by name, but in the city that would be impossible. It was nice that no one stared at her, but no one really looked at her either.

The girl came to another stone road, but the sign told her that the road headed west and not to Paradox. She kept walking and found the next road was the one she wanted. She was tempted to start down it at once, but as difficult as things had been with the merchants, she thought the road might have been more difficult without them.

So she looked for an inn or some sign of a group getting ready to travel the road to Paradox.

Chapter 12

Her journey along the road to Paradox was very similar to her journey from Ellsworth to Middlefort; only she traveled with a different caravan and had different duties. The second caravan she found was an extended family of merchants who took their children with them as they traveled. The girl was hired to keep the younger children occupied by reading to them from her history books. She liked this for it allowed her to ride in a large wagon with the children rather than make the entire journey on foot. Her goats and small wagon were tied by a length of rope to the back of the large wagon.

The family was loud and easy going. She shared her goats' milk, and they shared their food. At night, they told stories to each other around the campfire. One of the men played a lyre, and one of the women played a pipe. The others would improvise instruments and sing with them. The girl had had little exposure to the music made by men, but she found she liked it.

It reminded her of the nursery songs the old man would sometimes sing. He had never sung very well. His voice had been wheezy and untrained. He would often stop in the middle of songs or mumble through forgotten words, but it was not until she heard the family sing in clear, strong voices that she understood how badly he had done it.

One of the older boys tried for her attention, but he did it so clumsily she had no idea what he was doing.

The music made the girl miss playing with magic, but there was no time for spells. While the road was a little longer, time seemed to pass more quickly, and four days later, they arrived in Paradox.

Paradox was a hilly town, not as neatly laid out as Ellsworth had been. It possessed not a town square so much as a wobbly town trapezoid. More of the roads were paved or partially paved, and no one was fussy about having animals on them. There were extremely smelly little wagons whose drivers seemed solely dedicated to scooping up droppings and transporting them to pits outside of town.

The girl hoped they were paid well.

She said goodbye to the caravan that had brought her and began making inquiries about the flying caravan. She was relieved to learn that they were due to return from Laughing Peak any day now.

She also learned that flying was not a fanciful description. The flying caravan used a team of pegasus to fly over the desert to the mountain country of Uritz. The girl found this exciting but problematic. Her goats could not fly, and her books were heavy. The flying caravan was far more concerned with weight than their earth bound counterparts.

She made the difficult decision to sell her goats. They had been loyal friends and providers on her journey thus far, but she was not sure how long she might need to stay in Uritz. She could not bring herself to sell her books, even though they would bring her more money than the goats or wagon with the right buyer.

She bought a traveling pack and packed what she believed to be the most essential of items for a journey. The rest she sold or traded. She learned there were caves to the northwest of town and went searching until she found a small one that she believed she could find again. She wrapped her books in a sack and used magic to repel everything she could imagine might damage them.

She kept a book of magic for her traveling pack as it seemed the most useful thing to have, and she did not think she could live without something to read. She also kept her father's second journal to prove who she was.

Two days passed as she anxiously awaited the arrival of the caravan. To save money, she slept in the cave beside her books and walked back into town each morning to see if the caravan had come. On the third morning, she noticed several of the town's children making their way to a hill to the south. Curious, she followed them and soon learned that they too were anticipating the caravan's arrival.

It was midafternoon when the first farsighted child spotted the caravan in the sky. By then several adults had also come to join the crowd that gathered by the hill.

The caravan consisted of two large carriages, each suspended by six pegasus, three in front and three behind. They were tethered together by an odd network of ropes and widely spaced wooden yokes. There were smaller carts suspended between two pegasus each, and a few pegasus who were circling with riders but no other significant load.

They landed one by one, touching down at the top of the hill and taking a gradually slowing run to the bottom. The crowd had left a wide strip for them. The children cheered, and the adults applauded as each team made a successful landing.

The girl observed that the wings on these horses were much grander than the pegasus she had seen in Middlefort. The horses themselves seemed a bit smaller than those she normally saw pulling carts.

The caravan proceeded to the edge of town. The girl hung back as the carriages and carts were swarmed by eager townspeople. Some were merchants waiting for deliveries. Others were individuals in search of some trinkets not available locally.

The stars were out before the crowd left. A canvas had been stretched out between the carriages to shelter the tired pegasus. Some of the caravan's merchants had retired to the inn for the night, but others remained behind to guard the caravan. The girl watched them build a fire and move with purpose from task to task. The large man with a curly black beard was directing them, so she approached him cautiously.

"I wondered if you recalled a man named Mortagin?"

The large man scratched his beard thoughtfully. The girl was about to despair of getting an answer, when the man finally said, "Sounds familiar, but I can't place it."

"I think he may have traveled with you about twelve years ago. I'm told he had a short, stiff beard just starting to grey from brown."

The large man squinted at her. "Do you think I'm old enough to remember what happened twelve years ago? I was a young man, then."

The girl shrugged. "You're older than I am. Is there someone else, who might remember, traveling with you?"

The large man waved his hand and gave a short, loud laugh that made his beard bounce. "Just having a go at you, little skirt. I remember, though just barely. Left him in Uritz if I recall. Only remember because he prepaid for passage back and never took it."

The girl was encouraged by this news. "I'd like to go to Uritz," she said.

The black-bearded man shook his head. "Don't fly no girls. Wind kicks up their skirts too much. Nothing but trouble."

"Oh, I don't mind wearing pants," the girl said quickly. "And I don't mind working for my fare."

The bearded man laughed again and shook his head. "Run along, little girl. The skies are too rough for you."

"I've flown before," the girl said indignantly.

"But not with me, and nor will ya," the bearded man said. "No women folk is the rule, not even little ones like you."

The girl felt her face flush and stalked away. Silently she determined that she would somehow ride with the flying caravan to Uritz.

Chapter 13

The first thing the girl did was buy a pair of pants and boy's tunic with long sleeves. Since the tailor refused to fit them to her, she got a length of rope to tie them at the waist. She had always worn dresses because that was what the old man had bought for her. There had been no reason for her to think much about it. But she realized as she walked down the street that other people did think about it quite a bit. Women gasped when they spotted her, and men made remarks that were so cruel and crude she was more confused by them than offended.

The girl had changed into many things in her life, but she had never been a boy before. As she thought things over in her cave, she realized it was the only thing that would do. It was not just her skirt that the caravan leader had rejected; it was her gender.

Well, why not be a boy? she thought to herself. She supposed boys were just as good as girls. In her fairytale books, princes, soldiers, farmers, and tailors were just as often the heroes as the girls were. Maybe a little more so. The girl tried to think hard about boys she had seen close to her own age. It was enough of a change to pretend to be a boy instead of a girl than to pretend to be older too.

She flattened the little bumps on her chest, stretched her shoulders out a little broader, and shortened her hair. She snuck back into town and studied the boys there, copying noses and chins and hands. She did her best to look like a boy who had just finished school, thirteen or fourteen, a little awkward and gangly but strong enough to be useful.

With this new face and body, she went back and asked the large bearded man if he had work for her.

"You're in luck, lad," the large man said. "One of my riders has a wife in this town who's just about to give him their first child. He's wanting to sit out this flight, and I can't blame him. Good man. You ever fly before?"

"No," she admitted, doing her best to copy a boy's voice. "But I learn fast. Do you want me to ride?"

"Think I may swap you out with one of my inside men. Don't want to risk the pegasus."

"What does an inside man do?" the girl asked.

"You ride inside the carriage and make sure the cargo stays tied down," the bearded man said. "If things go wrong, you pull a cord which rings a bell, and I try to set down before there's damage done."

"I can do that," the girl said eagerly.

The black-bearded man looked over the lad before him. "I'll try you. We'll give you a few riding lessons before we leave. I like having some riders in reserve. It's a tough job."

The girl spent the next week at the camp of the flying caravan pretending to be a boy. She had wondered at first if she might be treated better as a boy than a girl but soon put that notion to rest. Different certainly, she was allowed and expected to do more, but people were far less patient and polite to her. While in essence they did the same sort of work that the merchants of her first caravan did, taking goods from one place to another, the men of the flying caravan were a little younger and thought of themselves as adventurers as much as merchants. She had fallen asleep to the sounds of the men in the first caravan discussing matters of money: how much they could charge, how much they might make, what sort of wares they should try to acquire for their return. In the flying caravan, everything seemed to be a competition: who had flown furthest, fastest, done the most of this or that. It really did not seem to matter what the subject was, only that one man could best another at it.

As she had never done most of the things they compared or done them very little, she was laughed at and ignored. They seemed to enjoy finding little ways to embarrass her. She tried to stay out of the way as much as possible and be accommodating, but her quiet and compliance seemed as easy for them to laugh at as anything else.

Even so, she could not help but be fascinated by some of their stories and felt a growing desire to have something of her own to brag about. The riding lessons began with a crash course in pegasus care. She learned why the pegasus she saw before had smaller wings. Cross breeding a pegasus was illegal in Uritz but common practice everywhere else. The flying caravan voluntarily complied with Uritz laws on the matter, both to show respect and maintain enough wings span for flight.

A pegasus saddle had extra straps, since there was greater danger in the rider falling. There were a few extra commands to learn, mainly "up" and "drop", which was different than the command to land. She had to tighten the leather around her thighs after mounting.

"These pegasus know the route," said the man training her. "You just need to stay in the saddle and keep your eyes open."

Her brief training involved not so much a flight as a particularly long jump from one hill to another. The pegasus liked to run with their wings out, which made for light feet and a relatively smooth ride. It was enough to make her understand why the men found flight so fascinating.

She also received a hasty education in knot tying. Everything on the caravan had to be tied down securely. "The Urites are a self-sufficient lot, so they don't import anything they need, only things they want," the black-bearded man explained when she asked what they were carrying. "They buy perfumes and glassware and other little fineries. We bring home pelts and metal work. Far more danger of things breaking on the way up than the way down, but lighter wares."

Uritz was a mountain country, and the girl was warned that higher elevation meant colder. She put the last of her money into a warm coat and hat.

Dawn broke on the day of the flight, and the girl ran around tying and double checking knots. Quietly she cast her own spells to make them more secure. Then she was rushed inside the largest carriage, where she would ride with the oldest man in the company.

There was a little wooden seat of sorts built into the side of the carriage and a place to tie a rope around her waist if she wished. She could not see much of the outside. There was a small glass window in the side of the caravan which was warped and would have been difficult to see through even if it was not half-covered by boxes. The carriage jostled and shook as they gained speed on the ground before taking flight. The girl gripped nervously wherever she could find a hand hold, while the old man chuckled at her.

The thought of flying had not scared her too badly; since the caravan had gone this route many times before, she had put her trust in the men who knew it. But in the air, every buffet and jostle reminded her that a fall promised death and most of the things that could go wrong were entirely beyond her control.

After a few hours without catastrophe, she began to relax. "What do you do if nature calls?" she asked the old man. He pointed to a small flap at the carriage's rear.

Slowly and with a growing sense of horror, she realized what it was for.

"Don't worry," the old man, seeing a lad's hesitation, but not fully understanding the source. "It's uninhabited desert below. You won't hit anyone."

The girl chuckled nervously, but said, "I think I can hold it." The men's lack of modesty with each other had surprised her more than a little, but she had always managed to turn her own head and look away. The old man shook his head but had the grace not to ridicule her.

The flight tested the patience of the girl's bladder, and the landing shook her considerably. It was more than a small relief to see the carriage door open and be allowed to untie the rope. She was allowed a few minutes to seek some privacy in the woods, before returning to help set up camp for the night.

The caravan would spend nearly a month in Uritz, trading and recovering from the intense flight. The riders were exhausted but recounted the details of the flight to each other before settling down to sleep.

While it had been a long day for her too, the girl found herself filled with nervous energy. She sat with knees to her chest and looked off the side of the mountain at the chirping, twinkling stars. Her father had come to Uritz the same way, but where had he gone?

Chapter 14

There were few places in Uritz that could be called a town. Moore's High was one of the larger settlements and only had a population to match the village where the girl had been born. No one had ever been able to make a proper count of the Urites. There were homesteads further up and down the mountainside, many impossible to find unless you already knew where they were.

Still wearing the face and form of a boy on the verge of being a young man, the girl helped feed the pegasus and unload one of the carts. When the company took a break for lunch, some of them walked into the village, and the girl went with them. It was nowhere near the cold bite of winter, but the mountain air was certainly cooler. The girl was glad to have her coat and hat.

The few people they passed on the road into town looked at her suspiciously, but their more disapproving looks were saved for the boisterous members of her party. The riders were well rested now and in better spirits. They jostled each other playfully as they walked and shouted hellos to familiar faces. Moore's High had no town square that the girl could determine, but there was a strip of shops, stands, and public buildings.

The view off the mountainside in the daytime was even more impressive than it had been from camp the night before. From the strip she could see the neighboring mountains and more spires beyond. Their tops white with snow, even though there were still months to go before winter.

The riders met some friends and turned into a pub. The girl followed even though her pockets were empty. She was hungry for something more than food. The men were clearly welcome in the pub. They shook hands, slapped backs, and sat in chairs the wrong way. The girl hung back while they ordered their drinks and food. When the party had settled into a loud but steady rise and fall of conversation, she quietly approached the bar.

"Not hungry, lad?" the bartender asked.

"No, I um..." she tried to keep her voice where the others would not hear her. "Do you know of a man named Mortagin?"

"Aye," said the bartender. "Thirsty?"

The girl shook her head. "I don't have any money with me. Do you know where he is? Or where he went? It would have been about twelve years ago."

The bartender grunted and began wiping the bar.

"Please, sir, I need to find him."

The bartender looked up and smiled. "Walk down the strip, and you'll find a path behind the candlemaker's. Follow that up the mountainside, and you'll find a Mortagin. Don't know if it's the one you're looking for, but he's been there about twelve years."

"Thank you, sir!" The girl hurried out of the pub and down the street, looking for the candlemaker. She found it, slipped through the narrow alley between it and the next shop, and found a dirt path that twisted up into the trees.

It was a bit of a climb. The path snaked through the trees. While not steep by mountain standards, it was more than she was used to. She spent the walk up trying to decide what to say to her father if she found him. After all, he might not even know he had a child, but at least she had his journal to show as proof. Unlike most people, her father would know about shifters, so he would not be surprised or frightened by what she could do.

She had expected to find a house at the end of the path, but instead the path ended at a gate and a stony clearing. There was no lock on the gate, so the girl swung it open. There were scattered trees between the stones, crooked but blooming with purple and pink blossoms. The clearing seemed to stretch around a stone outcropping and open onto a cliff where another fence had been erected for safety. The girl walked through, still hoping to see a house or a cave, but she had not gone far before the regular placement of the stones and etchings of names and dates made her realize she was in a graveyard.

There was no change in the weather, but the girl pulled her coat tighter and shivered. She walked slowly as she checked the names carved into the stone. Just around the outcropping at the base of a crooked tree, she found a little round stone with the name Mortagin carved into it.

She pulled her hat off her head and dropped to her knees. Somewhere in the back of her mind, she had known this was possible, even likely. But the death of hope is always a hard thing, as is the death of a parent. The tears came slowly at first but then harder until they were sobs.

The girl had thought she was all alone in the graveyard, but a low chuckle and the sound of footsteps interrupted her sobs. "Have some pride, man. Stop crying like a girl."

The girl looked up, vision blurred by tears. She blinked and saw a young man only a few years older than she was pretending to be, stepping down from a rugged sort of natural stair of stones by the outcropping.

"Are boys not allowed to cry?" she asked.

"Oh, a man may shed a tear, but only girls and infants cry with such abandon," said the young man in a teasing tone.

The girl was in no mood to be mocked. "If I told you I really was a girl, would you leave me in peace to grieve?"

The young man walked close and stood over her. He crossed his arms and looked down at a lad's face for the girl had not bothered to change it. "I started to say 'If you're a girl, you're the ugliest I've ever seen', but I realized that would be a lie. There's a girl back in Loch High with a harelip and a unibrow. She's hideous."

The girl did stopped crying, too stunned by the young man's audacity to think about her grief. He was the handsomest, most neatly dressed youth she had ever seen, but she wondered if he even had a heart. "Have you ever lost a parent?"

"No," the young man admitted. "But even if I did, I wouldn't cry like that. My father would be ashamed of me."

"Men are strange creatures," she said. "I bet you would feel like crying, even if you didn't."

"Maybe," the young man said, relenting a little and looking out over the cliffs. "Did your father just die?"

The girl wiped her eyes. "He died twelve years ago...but I just found out about it. I never got to meet him."

"That is sad," the young man said. "But hardly anything to cry over. After all if you never knew him, what did you really lose?"

"The chance to know him," the girl said. She stood and dusted her knees off. She might cry later, but she was not going to let this boy see her at it. "Why are you here, if not to grieve?"

"It's a pretty place," the handsome youth answered. "Climb up to the outcropping, and you'll get an excellent view." They had nothing else to say to each other, so the youth walked away towards the gate.

When he was gone, the girl climbed up to the outcropping. It was a pretty place, and if her father must be buried somewhere, she supposed this was as nice as any. She sat there for a long time, trying to decide what to do next. She had no money, and she was not eager to see anyone.

The youth was long gone, the graveyard deserted, so she took off her clothes and stuffed them into her traveling pack. When she had finished, she turned herself into large bird and took the strap of her pack in her talons. She let out a cry as birds cry and jumped into the air.

With the pack dangling beneath her, she flew off between the mountains.

Chapter 15

The girl made no attempt to keep track of time or direction as she flew. She let the wind carry her where it wished, rested when she was tired, but had no appetite for food. After a while, she began following the river because she liked the smell of it. The sun rippled on the slow current as it snaked its way through the mountain valleys. The elderly trees that stood sentinels on either side kept up a steady cadence. The fish played beneath the surface, singing burbling songs like schoolchildren.

Flying was not as tiring as walking had been. She flew high and spent much of her time gliding. Birds were shaped for such things. Miles of river passed beneath her with its smell of water and fish and trees and sun.

The arrow whistled by a good three feet past her, so there was a delay in her startled cry. She dove and dodged as a second followed it, less worried about the threat to her life than the fate of her precious books if they fell into the river.

She found shelter in the trees and changed there. Back in girl form, she slipped into her clothes and continued to follow the river on foot. The arrow meant there were people nearby or at least a person. While she was not yet eager to meet anyone, she did find her hunger was returning.

She knew worse come to worst she could probably catch a fish in the river or find an edible plant in the forest, but she had no experience fishing and little with edible plants and thought she would have better luck with finding food from people familiar with the area.

Four hours up the river brought her to the first signs of settlement, a pair of fishermen out on their boat. She called to them from shore, and after a shouted conversation, they rowed over to pick her up. The boat half-full of dying fish smelled terrible, but it was nice to be off her feet. The fishermen shared their lunch, and she sorted fish into barrels for them from her cramped seat.

When their work was done, they floated back downstream, and the girl fell asleep curled around a fish barrel.

The fishermen shook her awake when it was time to unload their barrels. They would not let her help with this task, but they did share their evening stew with her before pointing her towards town. Though the sky had begun to grow dark, the road followed the river, and her nap had given her energy. So she walked on. The girl picked up a stone by the riverside and sang a chant to it until it began to glow.

While she had changed the stone to light her path, looking at it made her realize that this was the thing she could do, and she determined that she would do it better than anyone else.

Perhaps not a difficult objective, given that her father had found no trace of people like her on this side of the sea, but maybe it was better to be unique. In a place where everyone could work magic, the ability would hardly be special. More readily accepted but more readily ignored.

By the time she arrived at the edge of town, many buildings had already dowsed their lights for the evening, but there was still light and noise at the local pub. She walked inside without drawing any attention and stole some bread from an abandoned plate.

While she sat there quietly chewing, a wobbly man smelling strongly of mead took the seat before her and said, "You're up late, little girlie."

Realizing how drunk he was, she decided to risk a game of her own. "I'm not a girl," she whispered. "I'm a fairy. Give me a coin, and I'll show you a magic trick."

The drunk pulled a coin from his pocket and placed it on the table. With a wobbly second thought he placed a thick finger on it before she could pick it up. "Show me the trick."

"Blow out the candle," she said, indicating the light on the table. The man did as told. With some quick words and a finger snap, she made the candle relight. It was still warm, so it was not a difficult bit of magic, but it made the drunk wobble back long enough for her to snatch the coin.

"Hey, Ma-arkrk! Mark!" the drunk called to his friend. "Come over, 'ere! Cum 'ere and seedis." But before the drunk could convince his friend to come over and turn back around, the girl had left the table and the pub.

She laughed and tossed her coin in the air. "Now, I'm a fairy," she said to herself. A moment later she yawned widely and asked herself, "Where do fairies sleep?"

That night the fairy slept on a haystack behind the barn.

She was chased off her bed in the morning by an annoyed stablehand. Picking hay from her hair, she went in search of a place to trade her coin for some breakfast. The coin bought her a small loaf from the bakers.

"Where am I?" she asked the baker, who gave her a funny look in return. "What's the name of the town?"

"Bow's Low," said the baker. "Though how you got here without knowing where it was is beyond me."

"Have you heard of a place called Loch High?" the girl asked.

"Aye, you're being a foreigner I take it?" said the baker.

"Aye, that I be," said the girl, mimicking the accent. "How would I get there?"

"Fly can you?" the baker asked, which was not as strange a question in Uritz as it may have been elsewhere. The girl giggled and nodded. "Follow the river west until you come to the great lake, then head north around the shore. I hear it's all up and down the mountainside. Hard to miss."

"Thank you," the girl said and took a large bite from her loaf.

"What business have you in Loch High?" the baker asked curiously.

The girl shrugged. "It's somewhere to go. Is it a big city?"

"Biggest in Uritz," said the baker. "I'd like to see it but don't like flying personally. And the rapids are too bad to go safely by river. Least that's what I hear."

"Would you give me some extra bread for my journey if I did some magic for you?" the girl asked.

The baker sniffed. "What can you do?"

"I could change the taste of the wood in your shop to chase away rats," the girl said.

"Be off, little beggar," the baker said contemptuously. "Do you take me for a fool?"

"Suit yourself," said the girl and walked away to finish her breakfast.

Chapter 16

Bow's Low was a sprawling town that had never experienced any sort of planning with its development. It ambled here and there on either side of the river. People flew from bank to bank on a pegasus or paid a ferryman for their passage. While it was fun for the girl to watch the pegasus hop the river, it was not an occupation that would provide food for her journey.

The girl had difficulty finding any customers for her more practical magic skills. The shopkeepers in Bow's Low did not trust outsiders and assumed she was looking to cheat them. She searched through her magic book for more showy ways to demonstrate her skills that would not frighten people. While the easiest thing for her to do was change herself, she had already learned that skill made few friends. Most magic was subtle or slow working and not good for quick demonstrations, but she could light candles and make rocks glow.

She found another pub and improvised a little show of glowing pebbles and candle lighting. Most of the Urites assumed these were clever tricks, but they were amused by them. The shows bought the girl dinner and a little extra for her trip.

She was sure Bow's Low was a reasonable place to live but found it a dull place to visit. By the next day, she had scraped together enough to pay a ferryman for passage down river, stopping short of the rapids. He looked at her curiously when she disembarked on foot but said nothing.

The girl walked along the river bank until she was sure she was far from anyone's view. She turned back into a bird and flew until she came in sight of the lake which the baker had told her about and others in the pubs had confirmed. Her pub customers had also told her that Loch High was the capital of Uritz where the king, the queen, and all the princes lived. This made her more curious to see the city, and she hoped it would mean richer clients for the new trade she was trying to create.

As eager as she was to reach Loch High, the arrow had taught her caution. At the first sight of a dwelling, she dropped back to earth and resumed her girl form. It would have been a very long and tiring walk, but she was lucky enough to meet a woodcutter who was taking a load to the city by boat. He was quite happy to let her move lumber and take a turn steering. She sang a spell that helped speed the little sailboat on its way, not a lot faster but a little bit. The woodcutter was very happy to reach the port earlier than anticipated. He laughed and said, if she stayed on to help him, he would be happy to marry her. "You're just a little twig now, but I imagine you'll grow into a proper tree."

She thought this far too funny a proposal to take seriously, thanked him for the ride, and quickly lost herself in the crowd at the docks.

She liked Loch High better instantly. It was the first time she had seen buildings in Uritz that took any concern over their appearance. Stone houses and shops zigzagged up the mountain side, some of them with actual glass windows and flower boxes. She walked without any particular destination, soaking up the sights and sounds and rhythm of the place.

She had been exploring the city for a few hours and had stopped at a stand devoted to the most colorful hats and scarves she had ever encountered, when she noted a ripple in the crowd. There was a young man walking down the street with four men in armor following. The young man walked casually, glancing curiously but with an air of boredom at the shops, as though hoping to spot something of interest but experiencing continual disappointment. The other pedestrians made way for him and bowed their heads as he approached.

The girl watched him curiously, but he paid no attention to her. He took his time passing, stopping to ask questions of various shopkeepers who answered him in a way that was both humbled and flattered. From their address, she came to understand that this was a prince. He was average height and lean build. His features were sharp and regular with straight brown hair just long enough to be impractical. He was dressed even more richly than he had been in the graveyard.

He was nearly to her when the shopkeeper hissed. "Bow your head, girl."

"No, I don't think I will," the girl said and crossed her arms instead. She was disappointed. Princes were supposed to be charming. The prince barely glanced at her as he passed. She almost let him go but found she could not stand the lack of recognition after what he had said to her. "I told you I was a girl," she said just loud enough for him to hear.

The prince snapped back around and looked at her curiously. He had intelligent brown eyes and a straight mouth. "When did you tell me that?"

"In the graveyard."

The prince stepped closer and leaned forward to

examine her face. For a moment, he looked a little worried, but soon his expression cleared and he laughed. "Tell your brother or whoever that it's a good trick, but I'm not falling for it."

"It's not a trick," she insisted.

"Has to be," the prince grinned. "I told the boy in the graveyard that he'd make an ugly girl, and you're too pretty."

The girl felt her face flush. The prince chuckled again and walked on. Before he had gone more than a few steps, she ran to catch up to him. "Where can I find the girl with the harelip?"

His brown eyes danced with surprise and amusement. "Did no one teach you to bow to your prince?" he asked.

"You're not my prince," she said.

"A traveler?" he guessed.

The girl nodded.

The prince lifted his chin and look down his nose at her. "And who gave you permission to come to my kingdom?" he asked.

"No one," the girl said uncertainly. "Do I need permission?"

The prince raised his eyebrows. "Are you here to start an invasion?"

"No," the girl said.

He narrowed his eyes shrewdly. "Spy? Assassin? Saboteur?" The girl shook her head, baffled.

"Are you a criminal? A grifter?"

"No."

The prince exchanged his mock concern for an easy smile. "Well, I suppose then I'll grant you permission for a visit. Be sure to spend lots of money and stay out of trouble, and if you don't bow for princes, I suggest you make an exception if you see the king."

The girl felt flustered and confused but could not help smiling. "And the harelip?"

"You are a funny one," said the prince. "You came all the way to the capital to ask a prince about a harelip?" While not entirely accurate, the girl nodded. "Heh, I try not to look at her, but I think she does some of the washing up at the castle. None of mine I hope."

"Why are you so cruel?" the girl asked.

"Cruel?" the prince repeated curiously. In a low voice, he said, "I could have your head cut off for not bowing or your tongue cut out for the lie. I thought I was quite merciful."

"I wasn't lying," the girl insisted, though her hand went nervously to her neck.

"Neither was I," the prince said and continued on his walk.

Chapter 17

The girl spent the next few days doing magic tricks in pubs to pay for food and a bed. She discovered Urites had a grand tradition of searching out an empty bit of mountainside and claiming it for their own. Property laws seemed to border on the nonexistent, though she heard the phrase "inhabit to hold" tossed about a fair bit in any conversation involving a legal dispute.

Sitting in a pub, she also came to learn of a cave recently vacated by a bear who had found the wrong end of a hunter's arrow. Since the hunter already had a nice little hut with a nice little wife, he said he had no use for it but thought it might make a nice hold for someone.

"I'll take it," the girl said.

The hunter gave her directions and walked her part way when he left the pub for home. The Urites believed trading for goodwill can prove more valuable than gold. The girl found the cave agreeable. It was much larger than the tiny one where she had left her books back in Gourlin but not so large as to be unmanageable, shallow enough to see the back from the mouth but deep enough to be a good rain shelter. There was a brook in walking distance and no shortage of trees nearby.

She spent her first evening gathering fallen twigs and branches to make a fire and exploring the minimal details of her new home.

The next day she returned to town and did her usual number of shows, but since she need no longer save her money for a room at night, she bought a thick mat and a few other little items to set up housekeeping. More chats in the pub explained that part of the "inhabit" aspect of "inhabit to hold" was to work some improvement on the land to make it more habitable, thus proving that you actually lived there and made use of the space. Claiming space you were not actively using was considered extremely tacky in Uritz and in some cases proof of madness.

She soon understood that Urites considered every one of their neighboring countries to suffer greatly from mental decline.

After much searching, she found a tiny little bookstore in Loch High. It was a claustrophobic space with books stacked on shelves all the way to the ceiling, most of them second hand. The girl loved it.

On a whim, she asked the owner if he had any books on magic. With a furtive look around the empty store and a secretive grin, the shriveled old bookseller brought some little tomes out from behind the counter. "I'm not supposed to have books on magic. Witchcraft is illegal you know, though there hasn't been a witch in Uritz in over a century. These came in a batch with a traveler. The man I bought them from claimed they are over three hundred years old, but that's impossible. The pages would be far more brittle than they are."

"Maybe someone used magic to make them last longer," the girl suggested. She gently touched the spine of one, and it seemed to sing a different tune than the other books in the shop.

The old man chuckled. "Well, I think it's all a bunch of

harmless nonsense for the most part. But I'm sure they're highly creative. If you want to buy them, I'll sell them very cheaply. Just promise me you won't tell anyone where you got them."

"Of course not," the girl promised.

Books were not valued as highly in Uritz. Uritz had no formal school system, so it was mainly nobility and merchants who had the ability to read and not all of them the desire. Even so, it took several extra shows, and a little creative gambling to pull together the money to buy the books.

Once the girl had the precious books, she holed up in her cave and read, or at least she tried. One book was a reference for potions and ingredients. Another was in a language she did not know, and the third was written in a very old form of Western Costal with lots of "ye"s and "thou"s, which slowed her progress. The fourth book was on witchcraft. The girl read a little of it but quickly realized that witchcraft and magic were very different things and that there was probably good reason for the former being banned.

Even so, she was glad for her treasures and wondered if other bookstores in other cities might hold similar relics of magic. The potions book proved very useful as it helped her identify plants, some of which she found in the forest and was able to sell to the herbalist. This trade with the herbalist allowed her to spend more time studying in her cave and acquire some little domestic comforts, jars and pots and thick blankets.

She was able to practice the magic she learned in the privacy of the woods. She learned the songs to make plants grow taller and healthier and used this skill to turn her stick fence into a true wall by growing vines to weave between the dead branches. Some of the branches had enough life left in them that she was able to coax them into spreading roots under the soil. She replanted some of the herbs she found closer to the cave mouth, so she could take clippings more easily. She was a lazy gardener, so the plants grew in wild patches.

It was nearly three weeks before she went to the castle to look for the harelip. She had been growing an idea this entire time, and she was ready to see if the harelip was game. She had learned from the pub talk that the prince's name was Leifhound, and she spotted him walking the grounds before she could find the harelip. This time she hid to avoid his notice.

The castle was a lively place. The domed towers were built from a yellowish stone, which gave it a golden look in the sunlight. It was set above the city and over to the side, though there were a few businesses and fine homes settled near it. There was a high wall of the same yellow stone surrounding the castle, but the gates stood open wide. Many well-dressed nobles and servants alike passed in and out.

On the far side of the castle was a wide creek and a sloping meadow. She found the harelip there among the other washing women. The women were busy with their work, so she sat and watched for a while. The harelip was a young woman with straight brown hair tied back with a thin scrap of twine. Beyond her deformity, she was a plain looking girl who dressed neatly and cleanly but took no special care with her appearance. She kept her face downcast out of habit and stayed close to an older woman who the girl guessed to be her mother.

They hung wet clothing on lines and as they dried, folded them into baskets. When the basket was full, one of the women would take the load back into the castle. The harelip's turn at this task came, and it was then the girl approached her and said hello.

The young woman with the harelip gave a gruff hello in reply and kept walking. The girl followed her into the castle. "Do you need something?" the young woman asked after she had set down her load.

"I was wondering if I could help you," the girl said quietly.

"I don't need anything," the young woman replied in the same gruff voice, still turning her face away out of habit.

"Please, let me show you something," the girl said. She waited until the hall had cleared around them, then split her own lip into copy of the harelip's mouth. The young woman's eyes widened, and she nearly stumbled over her own feet as she stepped back. "Watch," the girl ordered and returned her lip to its normal shape. "I think I could heal your lip if you'd like. Not as quickly, but if you'd let me, I'd like to try."

The young woman covered her lip with her hand. She looked very frighten, but behind the fear was a glimmer of longing. "You're a witch," she said. "Won't sell me soul for vanity."

"I don't want your soul," the girl said. She had hoped her offer would be better received. "I'll be honest, it's a bit of an experiment, but I really think I may be able to get your lip to grow. I won't *make* you do anything. I don't know exactly how long it will take. We can stop if you don't like it. But I would like to try."

The young woman looked slightly less frightened but confusion was replacing the fear.

"Why don't you think it over?" the girl suggested. "I'll come back tomorrow for your answer."

The girl left the young woman with the harelip and hurried home to her cave. The next day she returned as promised and met the young woman outside the castle walls.

"Me muther says I should let you try," the young woman said, still keeping her face turned down towards the ground. "It's not vanity mind you, but she thinks I'm more likely to get a husband. No man will marry a harelip. But she wants me to be sure of the price, says there's always a price, and I better know it 'fore I agree."

"No price," the girl said. "But if I succeed, I want you to tell people who's done it."

"There's always a price," the young woman with the harelip said skeptically.

The girl bit back a sigh. "Why don't you pay me by bringing supper with you every evening? We can eat together before I work on your lip. Is that a deal?"

The young woman nodded, and while it was hard to read an expression with her face turned away, the girl thought she looked a bit relieved. The girl waited and walked the young woman to the cave the first evening. After that she let the young woman come by herself.

Healing the lip turned out to be a simple if slow process. Most things preferred not to alter their natural state, but it was natural for living things to grow. Plants liked growing, so feeding their natural pattern was a simple sort of magic. Healing a harelip was very similar to growing a plant. The body knew how it was supposed to be. It had simply forgotten to finish growing and needed to be reminded. Every evening she tapped the edges to the split lip with her finger to wake them up, then she sang a chant to encourage them to grow. She made a salve from directions found in her new book and spread this on the lip to help with any discomfort the healing caused.

It was gratifying to see the skin grow in and feel the bone beneath knit and take shape.

The young woman, however, was a bit of a disappointment. The girl had hoped that gratitude and shared supper might lead them to become friends, but the young women with the harelip, whose perverse mother had named Haret, was an uneducated and dull person. Haret was grateful, but it was clear to the girl that she was still a little frightened of this cave witch. Even so, as her face improved, Haret did grow a little happier. She was faithful about bringing supper and held her head a little higher each evening.

It was two full weeks of work, but by the time they finished, Haret had a perfectly normal palate. She was still far from pretty, but Leifhound could not get away with calling her ugly anymore.

"Thank you," the young woman said, both smiling and sniffing away tears at the same time. "I was wondering, lady." Since the girl could give Haret no name, Haret took to calling her lady. "Do you think you could fix this too?" she asked, running her hand along her unibrow and looking guilty over the vanity.

"Oh," the girl said. "Well, I think you can just pluck those out or shave like men do."

Chapter 18

The girl had hoped that healing the harelip would bring her some wealthy clients with deeper purses. Her potions book was full of many little cures, and she liked the idea of getting paid and helping people at the same time. Still she had not expected her first client so soon. Being master of her own schedule, she slept in late and was just fixing her breakfast in the fire pit when Prince Leifhound burst through her open door.

"You?" he panted, looking rather flabbergasted. "You healed the harelip?"

The girl nodded apprehensively. The prince had the power to cut off her head after all.

The prince for his part narrowed his eyes and looked at her again like he had in the marketplace. "I wouldn't believe it, but I saw her. I made her tell me how it had been done. Is that why you were looking for her?"

"Yes," the girl said.

"And was that really you in the graveyard?" the prince demanded. "The hareli—the wash girl—"

"Haret."

The prince twitched but shook off this information as unimportant. "The girl you healed said you were a witch who could change your face."

"I'm not a witch," the girl said carefully. "But the rest is true."

"Show me," the prince demanded.

73

The girl looked down at the fire and stirred her breakfast. "I don't think I'm going to do it anymore. It scares people. I healed the harelip so people would see that magic can do good things."

"I'm a prince," Leifhound declared with crossed arms and a lift of his sharp chin. "I don't scare easily. I want to see your face change, or I'll have your tongue cut out for lying."

A sudden heat of anger made the girl want to scare the prince a little, so she changed her face into a copy of his own. The prince's eyes grew wide, then he smiled. "All right, I believe you," he said and squatted down so they would be eye level. "You are an odd one, aren't you?"

"You're not frightened?"

"Why would I be frightened?" the prince asked. "It is a little disconcerting to stare at one's self, though, particularly in a dress. I'm a handsome enough fellow, but I'd think it better if you were a girl again."

Feeling the rise of a different sort of heat, the girl changed her face back and took her breakfast off the fire.

"Can you look like anyone?" the prince asked, still watching her intently.

The girl nodded. "It's easier if I can see them. Sometimes I copy without realizing."

"Yes, I see," the prince said. "You kept a little of my eye and hair color. Don't you have a regular face of your own?"

The girl shrugged. "I don't think I've ever looked at myself," she said.

"What's your name, little witch?"

"I don't have one," the girl admitted, knowing this was another matter that usually unnerved people.

But the prince barely reacted. "Well, that's easy. I don't have to worry about forgetting it. I have a terrible memory for names. Gets me into awful trouble." He grinned, and she began to understand that most of what he said was only half-serious. "Tell me about the magic you can do."

While the girl felt some lingering reluctance to discuss the subject, the prince's attentiveness soon loosened her tongue.

"Oh, you are a treasure," he said, when she had finished. "I think you're right though. Common people might not appreciate your talents. They'll like cures for their colds well enough, but let's keep your face changing a secret between the two of us. Would you do that?"

Not sure what else to say, the girl agreed.

"Wonderful," the prince said. He began to look around her humble cave with an air of consideration and distaste. "You live here alone. No parents? No brother?" She said nothing in response and simply stared back at him until he remembered. "Oh, right. Well, don't worry. I'll take care of you now. I think I'm going to keep you on retainer. Do you know what that means?"

The girl shook her head.

"That means I'll pay you a nice monthly salary not to work for anyone else but me."

"You'll pay me not to work?" the girl asked.

"Oh, you'll have work just not all the time."

The girl frowned thoughtfully. "But what would I do with myself when I'm not working?"

"Whatever you want," said the prince, squatting down again. "I don't think you fully realize what sort of gift you have." The prince now examined her with the same look of consideration and distaste that he used to look over her cave. "When was the last time you had a new dress?"

"I don't know," the girl said, which was not entirely true,

but she did not want to discuss the old man's death with the prince. She had sold all but two of her dresses for the journey and supposed they were looking a little threadbare.

"Well, come along, let's go to the market."

The girl opened her mouth to object, but Leifhound held out his hand for hers. "Better douse your fire," he suggested. The girl spoke some quick words, and the fire went out. Leifhound's grin widened. "You are a wonder." He took her hand and pulled her along with him back towards town and the marketplace.

He released her hand when they came in sight of the townsfolk but was sure to keep her close. "This ragamuffin is offending my eyes with her shabby dress," he told the shopkeeper in an easy tone. "What have you got to make her presentable?"

In a blur of minutes, the girl found herself with a new dress in yellow tones that reminded her of the castle walls, and three more in red, green, and blue for later. They were not particularly expensive dresses, but they were new and well made, appropriate to a successful tradesman's daughter. The prince went on to buy her two pairs of new shoes, which she sorely needed, and a hair ribbon which she didn't. He carried no money with him but told each merchant to send the charge up to the castle.

"Isn't it strange for you to walk around without an escort?" the girl asked, when they stopped for lunch.

Leifhound laughed. "My mother doesn't like it, but father doesn't mind. I usually take the escort out when I want to be noticed. Formal inspections and informal tours, that sort of thing. Loch High is a fairly safe city, particularly if you stick to the crowds and main roads. Besides, I'm the oldest of seven brothers, so I'm expendable. It's not like in

Cordance where they have only one prince. I hear he's hardly let out of his mother's sight. Then again, what is he now... ten? I wouldn't let my ten-year-old brother run about the marketplace unescorted. Really only the last couple years I've been allowed."

He took her inside a hat shop and placed a purple cap with a red feather her head. "That suits you."

The girl could not help smiling from the attention. It had been a long time since anyone had bought her something. "What sort of work will I be doing?" she asked, when they left the shop and headed back in the direction of the castle.

"Oh, this and that," Leifhound said. "You strike me as fairly versatile. I'd just much rather have you on my side, before someone else takes you on theirs."

"Do you have enemies?" the girl asked.

"Not that I'm aware of," the prince said. "But I'm in line to be king, and a king needs to take precautions to keep his crown."

"Is that why you want me to be a secret?"

"You understand me," Leifhound said, as they came in view of the castle. He stopped and his eyes grew distant. "Little witch, I have a strange favor to ask of you."

"Is this part of my job?" she asked, eager to be useful.

"No, no," the prince said slowly. "It's a personal favor, but I think it might save me from madness."

Intrigued, the girl looked up at him curiously. "What do you want me to do?"

Chapter 19

Prince Leifhound did not answer right away but led the girl towards a grove of trees for privacy. There were a few large rocks among the trees, and he sat down on one of them. "Might be a bad idea, but I'm going to ask anyway, since you're the only one who could possibly help me."

"I'm listening," the girl said, taking a seat beside him on the rock.

The prince spoke in a low voice. "You see there's this girl I'd really like to kiss, but I can't because she's promised to another man."

"How can I help with that?" the girl wondered. She knew no magic spells for changing hearts.

"You can make yourself look like her, and then I can kiss you."

It was late afternoon now, and the low sun on the tall trees cast long shadows. "You wouldn't really be kissing her then," the girl pointed out.

One of these long fingers of shade crossed the prince where he sat, casting him half in light and half in shadow. "No," he conceded easily. "But I figure it's the next best thing."

"What does she look like?" the girl asked.

"Come with me," the prince said eagerly, taking her hand again. "I'll show her to you." Despite his earlier wisdom on sticking to crowded areas for safety, Leifhound led her through a series of back alleys. He stopped behind a retaining wall. While the wall was fairly short from their side, it dropped considerably on the other. Sounds of a gathering floated over the wall. The prince crouched down so he could peek through a break in the stones and indicated for the girl to do the same.

It was indeed a gathering, though the girl could not discern the exact nature, perhaps a family affair as there was a range of ages present.

"There she is," the Prince said. "The blonde one in the middle by the clothes line."

The girl spotted the blonde in question, who was quite beautiful. She was sandwiched between two other young women, both fairly attractive themselves and laughing. "What's her name?" she asked.

"Merit," Leifhound sighed. He looked sad when he said it, and it was the first time the girl had ever seen anything make him sad.

The girl stared down at the blonde and, partly to protect Merit's smile, partly to ease Leifhound's sadness, and partly because she was a twelve year old girl who thought it might prove nice to be kissed by a handsome prince, copied her form. "Will this work?"

"Perfect," Leifhound declared. He snatched her hand and pulled her away quickly, she supposed to a place they were even less likely to be seen, nestled in an alley of high walls. "Can I kiss you now?"

"If you like," the girl said.

The prince did, and it was very unsatisfying for both of them.

"You're right," he said. "It's not the same. You need to change again before someone sees you."

The girl did, though this time she left her hair a little blonder. "Why did you want to kiss her?"

"Because she's the most beautiful woman I've ever seen," Leifhound sighed as they walked back towards the castle. "She has a laugh that puts wings in my chest, and she's the sweetest girl I've ever met in my entire life. I keep dreaming about her."

"If you really love her, why not tell her?" the girl asked. "I know she's engaged, but she isn't married yet."

Leifhound scowled, though not at her. "Because I can't offer her anything. I'm a prince. I have to marry someone with political connections. The baker's daughter won't do. If I told her how I felt, it wouldn't accomplish anything. At best she'd laugh at me; at worst it would make her miserable and ruin her marriage."

The girl thought this over. "Did you really think kissing a copy would help?"

The prince shrugged. "I thought it might help me stop thinking about it." He picked up a stone from the pathway and threw it. "My father's down south right now trying to arrange a marriage for me to that Tivin princess with the silly name."

"I take it you don't like her."

"Oh, I'm sure she's a fine girl," Leifhound said. "But she's five. Tivans have a marrying age of nineteen. I'm not in the biggest rush to get married, but I don't want to wait fourteen years either. I'm practically a man now. I tried to convince father to arrange it for one of my brothers. Huntsen's six. Coiler's four. They'd be the least inconvenienced. But father's convinced that the Tivans will want the eldest son."

For the first time, the girl felt a little sorry for Leifhound. "Maybe they'll take the second eldest brother, so he can be king there and you here."

Leifhound laughed. "I hope not. Dolfe's an idiot. He'd make a terrible king. Pieter would be the best choice. He's brilliant, only ten but a regular scholar. But he's the fourth son, smack in the middle, which means no one notices him."

"That seems unfair."

"It would be," Leifhound agreed. "But I think Pieter likes going unnoticed. As I said, he's very smart."

The girl took Leifhound's hand to comfort him and herself. He allowed her to hold it until they came back in sight of others. "I have to think things over tonight," he said. "But I'll come back for you tomorrow."

Chapter 20

The next day Leifhound came for her early in the morning again and took her back to the castle. Instead of going through the gate, he took her around the back where the wall met the mountain. "I go this way when I want to sneak in and out unnoticed," he said. "Not that I really need to. It's more of a game. But I can't very well take you to my room through the front gate."

Leifhound came to a spot where the stones were uneven and began to climb the wall. "Come along. That's my window."

The girl knew enough of the world to hesitate. It is generally unwise for a girl to follow a strange boy into his room, particularly if he has to sneak her in through the window. But most girls can not turn into a bear or an eagle if a prince decides to be unprincely, so the girl had less reason to fear for her safety than most. She followed behind the prince using the same foot holds, and he lifted her inside when she came within reach.

"Why bring me here?" the girl asked.

"For the mirror," the prince said, pointing to a vanity with a large if somewhat clouded mirror. "I think it important you have a face of your own; otherwise, you'll draw the wrong sort of attention."

There were lingering traces of Merit and Leifhound in the face that stared back at the girl.

"Do you take a little bit of everyone you meet with you?"

the prince asked.

"Doesn't everyone?" the girl asked.

The prince smiled. "Perhaps, but not so obviously. Most of us carry the people we know inside."

"Most people look like their parents," the girl said, realizing that she had no true image of them, not even in her own face.

"You could be the most beautiful woman in the world if you wanted," said Leifhound, pulling her hair back, so they could see her face clearly. "But I think a plain face might serve you better. I've been trying to think of the best way to install you in the castle and get you out of that cave, but it'll be easier if you don't draw too much attention."

"I like my cave," the girl protested. "It's mine."

Leifhound laughed. "Now you're starting to sound like a Urite. You realize having a hold makes you a citizen, which makes me your prince. You ought to bow your head to me now."

"You kissed me. I am not going to bow to you," the girl said stubbornly.

"As you like," the prince said, placing a second kiss on her temple. "A price for your silence. But I will insist you bow to my mother and father; we'll both live longer that way."

"Would your father really hurt you if I didn't bow?" the girl asked.

"Probably not," the prince conceded. "But if I make him angry enough, he could disown me or throw me in prison. Then we'd have Dolfe for a king, and the whole land would suffer."

"Do you want to be king?" she asked.

"Eventually. Why wouldn't I?" Leifhound asked.

"So you could marry Merit," she said.

Leifhound sniffed. "One can learn to love the wife they have. It's not like in fairytales where you have to go questing for it, or romances where there's only one girl in the world who could possibly do. At least I'll always be rich and important, and that's nothing to sneeze at. A poor man might not be able to marry for lack of funds, and heaven help him if he falls in love with a noblewoman. Everyone has their restrictions. Except for you, you could have anything you wanted."

The girl looked at the prince askew. "I don't have any of the things I really want."

"What is it you really want?" Leifhound asked, pulling up a stool to sit beside her. "I'll get it for you."

The girl thought of the mother who had left her, the old man who had died, and the father who would never give her a name, but even a prince had natural limits. So she thought of the only thing left that brought her joy. "Books."

"I'll see you have a library," Leifhound promised. "But first we need you to make a face you can call your own."

They spent well over an hour before the mirror, trying different colors and features. The girl started to make herself look older like Merit, but Leifhound advised her against it. "Let's learn from Pieter and try to avoid attention for now. A single twelve-year-old girl is not an oddity. A single eighteen-year-old girl who isn't hideous begs for suitors, and a pretty one always causes trouble."

At length they found features that suited her, but Leifhound did not like her choice of hair color. "The curls are fine, but you're not a blonde."

She could not resist teasing him. "But you like to look at blondes."

"No, I like to look at a particular blonde, and I don't need you reminding me of her," Leifhound said. "But that's beside the point. You, little witch, are not a blonde. Try auburn." She humored him. "There, that's perfect. You're pleasant to look at but not too distracting, and we can let you grow into quite a beauty. Plenty of pretty girls are gawky at twelve."

They sat a little longer, so the girl could try to memorize the face they had made. Brown eyes and auburn hair, pleasant but unremarkable features. When she was sure she could remember it, they climbed back out the window and down the wall. "Don't you worry about burglars or assassins?" the girl asked.

"Not really," the prince said. "It's not obvious you can climb up until you're right under the window. I bar the shutters from the inside when I don't want visitors, and I figure anyone who scales the wall to steal my hairbrush needs it more than I do. If they go past my room, they'll run into the guards who walk the halls. Besides, the front gate is usually open, so a thief could walk in that way easier than he could scale the back wall."

"Do I get to walk in the front gate next time?" the girl asked.

"This afternoon," Leifhound replied. "I'm going to take you to meet our magician."

"You have a magician?!" the girl exclaimed, more than a little surprised by this revelation.

Leifhound was less enthused. "The king of Cordance had one, so father thought we ought to. He's ridiculous, but I think now you've given me a use for him."

Chapter 21

That afternoon Leifhound took her to meet the castle magician. The magician was an average looking man, too old to be called young and too young to be called old, who dressed in bold, bright colors and an excessive amount of fabric. The prince's visit caught him off guard, and the magician scurried about his chamber trying to pack away tools of his trade that had been left lying about.

"You have no apprentice, correct?" Leifhound more stated than asked.

"Correct, Highness," the magician said, bobbing his head in a series of hasty bows.

"Good, I have one for you," Leifhound announced, surprising both magician and girl.

The magician twisted his hands. "Highness, please, a magician's secrets..."

Leifhound laughed. "I don't expect *you* to teach *her* anything, but she'll be a credit to you all the same."

The magician was not so easily convinced. "Prince Leifhound, I can't take a girl for an apprentice. What would people say? What would your father say?"

"My father left me in charge, Clythe, so take my word as his until he returns to contradict me." The prince had no laughter in his voice now.

"But Highness, where will she sleep?" the magician asked.

"In my cave," the girl said resolutely.

"As you like," Leifhound agreed with only the slightest hint of disappointment. "As long as you're here every day."

"As you like," she returned. "But we've yet to discuss my salary."

"Oh, right," Leifhound said thoughtfully. "Twenty gold per month?"

The magician surprised expression grew to one of pure disbelief. "Highness, I only receive five."

"Plus room and board," the prince reminded him. "Frankly, I think you're a waste of income, but humor me on this, and you'll keep your room even when my father passes."

Disbelief stewed into indignation which soured into suspicion. "Oh, I see…" the magician said bitterly.

"You see nothing," the prince snapped at him. "*This* is the girl that cured the harelip."

The magician looked at the girl with fresh eyes. "Ah, I offer my apologies, Highness, young lady. That's a different matter."

Satisfied, Leifhound bid them good day. "Believe it or not, I do have other things to do than get you settled."

Once he had gone, Clythe the magician encouraged the girl to close the door, so they could talk. "I've worked out how you did it," he said once she had taken a seat across from him at his work table. "Your *healing* of the harelip."

"You've really studied magic then?" the girl asked.

"Oh, exhaustively," chuckled the magician. "Beautiful but gutsy little trick. You've even got Leifhound convinced."

The girl felt her brow knit with confusion. "I'm sorry; I don't follow."

"The harelip was a modest girl who always kept her head down and did what she could not to draw attention," the magician explained. "Even when people looked at her, all they really saw was that unsightly gash. You found a girl, about the same height and build, and bribed her to take the harelip's place." The girl opened her mouth to object, but the magician continued. "Maybe you did everyone involved a good turn. Maybe the replacement wanted a nice steady castle job; maybe the harelip wanted an excuse to go into hiding. I'm pretty sure you bribed the mother with gold, but maybe she can hold her head a little higher now that her 'daughter' is no longer deformed.

"And your trick has worked well so far, secured you a spot in the palace. But I'd be careful not to overplay your hand with Leifhound. You have him convinced right now. Could be your head if he ever figures it out, though."

The girl's mouth still hung open, but even when the magician stopped talking, she could find no words.

"Close your mouth, little grifter. You'll only catch flies that way. Despite what the prince says, I think I'll call you my assistant rather than my apprentice. I don't doubt you're clever to pull off a trick like that, but a man must watch his reputation. And no respectable man takes a little girl on as an apprentice." The magician studied her for a moment, then pulled out a deck of cards. "Since I'm stuck with you, let's see if you can do a proper fortunetelling."

"But fortunetelling isn't magic!" the girl protested.

"Not exactly," the magician admitted. "Though you must admit both are about letting the audience fool themselves. There's something about the feminine mystique. People like their fortunetellers to be women, and their magicians to be men."

"But magician just means magic user...it's not gender specific."

"Don't confuse reality with perception, girl," the magician said, making a coin appear with a flip of his hand. "Magic is all about bending the perception to create a reality for the audience more wonderful than the real world." He closed his hand, and the coin was gone when he reopened it. "Now what's your name?"

At first, the girl thought the magician must be a rather great wizard to make coins out of air, but she soon came to realize that he preformed no true magic at all, only sleight of hand tricks. He did do a little chemistry, which is similar to magic, but even that was done to enhance an illusion with little fires and puffs of smoke.

To say the girl learned nothing from him might be unfair, but it was certainly not the sort of magic she had been hoping for or expecting.

She found the prince later and told him sulkily. "He thinks I'm a fraud."

"Men like to see themselves in others," Leifhound joked. "May as well let him think it for a while."

The girl was not appeased. "He's not a real magician at all. He only does tricks and knows nothing of magic."

Leifhound smiled in a way that said he was already well aware. "I did say he was ridiculous, but it gives you an excuse to hang about the castle, which is the important thing. Forget him and come with me, little witch."

"I'm not a witch," she corrected but followed him anyway.

Leifhound led her to a small backroom of the castle. "Here's the library I promised." It was not a large library for a castle, only a few shelves along one wall, but they were well stuffed with books. "Not yours exclusively. It'll take time to build your own, but this is the educational library for me and my brothers. You're welcome to any of the books here, though I ask you take them one at a time and return them as you finish."

"Thank you," the girl breathed. If she did nothing but read she might finish all the books within a couple of years, but it was still a welcome and generous gift.

"Have you ever handled a baby before?" Leifhound asked from the doorway as the girl took a book from the shelf and cradled it.

"No," she admitted.

Leifhound smirked. "Well, tomorrow you'll learn and start earning your keep."

Chapter 22

She met Leifhound the next morning by the castle gates. He took her inside to a grand bedroom, where a richly robed and lovely woman with long dark brown hair and tired dark brown eyes was lying back, propped up into a sitting position on an enormous bed. "Hello, mother," Leifhound said, giving the queen a kiss on her pale cheek.

Without being prompted, the girl dropped into an awkward curtsy. Not just because this woman was a queen, but because she was a mother. In the queen's arms was a small, swaddled babe peeking at them through slitted eyes.

"Are you better today?" Leifhound asked.

The queen briefly touched the jaw of her eldest before returning her hand to coddle the infant. "I'm tired from nursing, but there's no pain," the queen said in a voice of such perfect tone and dignity that the girl felt rather humbled.

"Mother, this is the girl I told you about," Leifhound said to introduce her.

"Hello, girl, I'm glad Clythe could spare you," the queen said with a weary but gracious smile. "You have experience with infants?"

"Mother," Leifhound interrupted. "Let me worry about Michter. You need to rest." With a little reluctance, the queen allowed Leifhound to take the baby. He held his littlest brother securely in one arm, took an extra blanket from the cradle beside the bed with another, and with a slight tilt of his chin telling the girl to follow, left the room.

The girl saw that the queen was nearly asleep before they were out the door. A nurse who had been sitting quietly at her bedside moved to smooth the queen's hair and check her brow. Since Leifhound had his arms full, the girl gently closed the door.

"Is she...?" the girl began and stopped, afraid to give voice to her concern.

"Oh, no, she'll be fine," Leifhound assured her. "She grows stronger everyday, but I do suspect this will be the last prince of Uritz." He laid the blanket over the girl's shoulder. "If you can hold Michter with half the care you showed that book yesterday, we should be fine. Be gentle, but keep your arms strong, and always support the head."

Leifhound laid the baby carefully against the girl's shoulder and showed her how to move her hands to support it properly. "Is this my work?" the girl asked. "I told you I know nothing of babies."

"You'll learn quick enough," Leifhound said. "Besides, I know how to care for him. I just need you to hold him, so I can keep my hands free. Come along, let's collect my other brothers."

The infant prince, recently fed and clean, snuggled contently against the girl's shoulder. Dolfe, Angsfel, and Pieter who were fifteen, thirteen, and ten needed no more than a word to collect them for a trip to the meadow, but Huntsen and Coiler, six and four, proved more of a challenge. Leifhound used his free arms to gather up little Coiler, while Dolfe plucked Huntsen off the dresser.

Once they were outdoors, the little princes ran for the gate under their own power. The girl followed as quickly as she could while taking care with the baby and shading his eyes from the sun as Leifhound directed her.

They passed the washing women and crossed a wooden bridge to the large expanse of sloping meadow beyond. The young princes ran like rabbits freed from a cage, darting here and there. Angsfel and Pieter were soon swatting at each other with wooden swords while Dolfe chased after Coiler. Leifhound led the girl to sit in a place by the tall grass. Keeping half an eye on his brothers, he showed her how to offer the baby a finger to hold.

"We have other nursemaids, but they work in shifts," he explained. "Once Michter starts sleeping through the night, I think mother will be fully well and not need the extra help, but she's not had a full night's sleep yet since the birth."

The girl found she did not mind so much. Little prince Michter was teaching her the delights of babies.

"I thought this was a nice solution for the short term," Leifhound said. "It allows me to keep you close without drawing attention. No one takes too much notice of the nursemaid."

"Aren't you running things with your father gone?" the girl asked.

"Not really," said Leifhound, tickling Michter, who made a delightful little sound. "We have a steward who runs things."

"So you just spend your days lounging in meadows?"

"I spend my days helping my mother look after my six younger brothers, and while my father is gone, I stand in for him at official functions. There are my own studies of course, though I've reached a point where I mainly study as I need and please." Leifhound took Michter in his arms and spoke softly. "It may not seem like work to you, but I am the heir to the throne with six younger brothers who might gain a crown if I met a misfortune. Kingdoms are torn apart with such dark games, so this play and bonding is important. I figure my brothers are less likely to rise against me if I treat them well, and they have childhoods full of fond memories with me. How do you wish harm on someone who changed your diapers, tended your scraped knee, or taught you to fire a bow?"

The girl considered this and saw the wisdom in it. "Perhaps you should speak more kindly of Dolfe then?" she suggested.

Leifhound smiled. "Dolfe makes no pretense of being a scholar, but I promise you I do treat him well. He and I have talked extensively about what his future role might be. There are benefits to being the beloved brother of a king or future king. I'm planning to make him Captain of the Guard. He's not the sort of clever that ought to be running a country, but he's a fine swordsman and archer. He's tall, which forces men to look up to him. I think he'll make a fine Captain, and I'll keep him close and see to it he's comfortable."

"And Angsfel?"

"Too young to cast in a definite role, but I think maybe an ambassador."

"Pieter?"

"An advisor, possibly my new steward when the current one retires."

"Huntsen?"

"Now, you're trying to cast me in the role of fortuneteller," Leifhound said in his laughing way. "Do you begin to understand what the job of the king is?"

"To rule people," the girl guessed.

Leifhound shook his head. "Maybe elsewhere, but Uritz is a country of free men who do not like to be ruled. No, in Uritz, the king acts as the ultimate judge. He settles disputes that can not be handled by local magistrates and oversees foreign affairs. But my father says the real job of the king is to make sure he has the best people for each job. The steward runs the family holdings, but the king appoints the steward and removes him if he fails at the post. No one man could possibly run a kingdom, so the king's true job is delegation."

"Then why do men bow to you?"

"Respect," Leifhound said. "The king must be a wise and discerning man. If he fails at his job, there will always be someone happy to remove him from it."

"And are you wise, Leif?" she asked, trying out the nickname.

He grinned at her presumption. "Perhaps not yet, but I do fancy myself as discerning."

"How so?"

"I can read a person's character in their eyes," he bragged. "I always know when someone's lying to me."

"But you accused me of lying," the girl pointed out.

"I remember," he said and handed the baby back to her. "I made the mistake of trusting the facts rather than myself. I was very glad to be wrong."

"Trusting the facts?"

Leifhound lay back on the grass, stretching out with his hands laced behind his head. "Well, you didn't look anything like the boy in the graveyard. No amount of makeup or costume could explain the difference, so I took it as evidence of a lie."

A smell caught the girl's attention, and she wrinkled her nose.

"I was glad to be wrong about you," Leifhound said with his usual grin. "It proved I was right."

95

The girl realized the smell was coming from the baby, which led to another realization; princes poop.

Chapter 23

The girl turned thirteen while she was in Uritz though she had long ago lost track of her birthday. The Elder had come from a generation that counted age by winters rather than specific dates.

Leifhound was right that people paid little attention to her while she held the baby. He was able to keep her close and speak little remarks under the pretense of attending his baby brother. The queen held the child more and more herself as her strength returned. While the girl enjoyed her time with baby Michter, she did not mind his return to his mother. This left her free for other things.

Leifhound taught her to dance, though he did not dance with her himself. Angsfel was shy a partner at a birthday party for the steward's daughter, and she was the right height to fill in. Angsfel was fairer than Leifhound, nearly blonde like Dolfe and Coiler. He was also closest to the girl's age and had the most beautiful face she had ever seen on a boy, but he was cold in manner and held little attraction for her.

Pieter discovered her limited knowledge of the Southern and Eastern Mountain tongues and came to her for study help with his languages. In turn, he introduced her to books on the ancient tongues. Pieter had the darkest hair of the brothers, most like his mother. She liked him, but it was Leifhound's company she sought.

She found herself hanging on Leifhound's every word,

even when he spoke nonsense. She noticed he was far more polite to courtiers than he had ever been to her. She scolded him about it, which amused him. "But with you, little witch, I'm always perfectly honest. Isn't that better?"

While she rankled over it, she decided it was.

He took her on a hunt with the premise of keeping an eye on Huntsen and taught her how to shoot a bow. Her aim was imperfect, but she found a spell to better it. She cherished the warmth he had left on her hand during the lesson. He seemed to forget Merit, though he worried more and more about the news his father might bring with his return. While he did not speak of love at all, she believed his little touches, a ruffling of hair, a playful tap on the nose, a guiding hand on her shoulder, spoke some affection. She laughed with him, argued with him, and hoped he would kiss her again as herself but dared not ask him to.

The possibility of engagement to the little Tivin princess hung over both of them like a dark shadow, and the girl prayed that the Tivans had accepted a younger brother in Leifhound's stead.

She climbed up to Leifhound's room sometimes to practice faces in his mirror. He always welcomed her, though he often lay on his bed reading until she left. While his humor was sometimes cutting, he was never unprincely. Her own tongue grew sharper to keep up with him.

She climbed up to his window late one day to find him absent from the room. Before she could settle herself at the vanity or check the bedside to see what book he was reading, Leifhound flung the door open. And before she could apologize for the intrusion, he closed the door, caught her up, and planted an enthusiastic kiss on her forehead.

"Father's just sent word from Snow Port," he said giddily.

"The Tivans wouldn't take any of us. The little princess's grandfather thinks she's far too young for an engagement. Shrewd old man, probably waiting to see if his son can manage a proper heir."

"So you're free to choose your bride now?" the girl asked.

"I'll have to wait 'til father gets home to know that," Leifhound said. "But at least I shouldn't have to wait fourteen years. That, my darling, might be unbearable."

He had too much energy to sit still, so they climbed down the wall and up the mountainside (Leifhound loved climbing) to do some stargazing. He allowed her to sit close and put an arm around her shoulder while he pointed out constellations.

She would have happily spent the night under the stars, but he made her climb down when she started yawning. "We don't want to worry anyone."

Chapter 24

Leifhound's father returned in a foul mood, though that was soon lightened by little Michter. There was a grand ball to celebrate the king's return, and the girl was able to attend as the baby holder. She had hoped the king might give her a favorable look since she had become so close to his sons, but as best she could tell, he did not see her at all. The queen spoke kindly but never asked her about anything that did not have to do with the baby.

She watched Leifhound dance with the well-dressed ladies and hugged Michter close until the queen asked for him. For the first time, discontent blossomed inside her. She wanted Leifhound to speak to her and kiss her forehead openly and publicly. She wanted to call the queen mother too.

Though the weather was beginning to grow colder, the princes were out the next day on the meadow. Even baby Michter was bundled in extra layers. They spread a blanket on the ground for him so they could encourage him to try sitting. Leifhound ran with his younger brothers and bested Dolfe in a wooden sword duel before coming to sit beside the blanket.

"Father told me last night he has no specific plans for marrying me off," Leifhound confided, while he watched his brothers investigate an animal burrow further down the hill.

"Does that mean you'll have your pick?" the girl asked.

"My pick of girls who'll have me," Leifhound replied in his usual good humor. "Believe it or not, there are girls who would turn down a prince's offer. There are some girls at court who don't like me. I had trouble remembering their names, and they took offense. They probably are horrified at the idea of being married to such a careless husband."

"I think it would be nice to be your wife," the girl said softly.

The prince laughed. "Oh, you'd be a fun wife. Never boring," he said before looking at her. "You're too young to be thinking about marriage, little witch."

"I'm not that young," she said, propping up little Michter. "And I'll grow. Is it wrong to admit I'm fond of you?"

The prince's smile grew rather fixed. "I thought you understood." He leaned towards her, though his brothers were still on the other end of the meadow and there was little danger of being overheard. "I'm the eldest son. I may have some options now, but I have to make a marriage that's politically favorable. A nameless girl with no father wouldn't do, even if you were the proper age."

The girl said nothing, but the prince saw her disappointment. "Don't worry. We'll still see each other every day. I told you I'd take care of you, and I will. It's my plan to raise your station, but I turn eighteen soon. I'd like to be married by twenty. That may sound impatient, but consider that, until I have an heir, Dolfe is next in line to the throne. He will make a fine Captain, but I truly believe a terrible king. If I could name Pieter, I would, but after Dolfe, there's Angsfel and...I'm uncertain what sort of man he will be.

"Besides, I told you a king's job is to get the right people in the right jobs. And you, my dear, would be wasted as a wife."

She gave him a glare that demanded explanation.

Leifhound reached a hand down to play with Michter as he often did to cover the fact they were talking. "Little one, do you even understand what a wife does for her husband?"

"I know what a wife does," the girl said shortly.

Leifhound looked at her skeptically. "A wife bears her husband's children and manages his household. An unfortunate woman must manage her husband as well. A queen's household is larger than most. She has other duties to support her husband, acting as hostess and diplomatic support. My mother oversees the education of her seven sons, and five to seven children is considered an average sized family in Uritz. I know women with thirteen and twenty. Do you think they have time for their own study? Or to work a trade? A queen is a manager, and your talents would be wasted in that position."

"You think I couldn't do it?" the girl asked. "Or that it's not an important job?"

"It's an extremely important job," Leifhound agreed easily. "I have the highest respect for my mother, and I'm quite sure you could handle it. However I do not have such a low opinion of women to think you're the only one. Many women are very good managers. But you have unique skills and knowledge that would be of very little benefit to a queen. You're a healer, who can change her face at will. I can think of a thousand fantastic things only you could do. Would it be wise of me to take you away from them to manage a household, which another woman could do just as well or better?"

"Would you have me never marry?" the girl asked.

Leifhound frowned thoughtfully. "I'd prefer it. It's not

like you need a husband to care for you."

"You don't think a woman might want a husband, the way a man wants a wife, for reasons other than necessity?" the girl asked indignantly.

"I suppose," Leifhound conceded. "But you would chafe under the yoke most men place on their wives."

"Are you most men?" she snapped.

Leifhound disarmed her with a compliment. "See how clever you are? I can't contradict you without humbling myself. Though perhaps I'm not so extraordinary as you think me."

The girl pretended to be preoccupied with the baby, but Leifhound lifted her chin to make her look at him. "I have no doubt you could gain the sort of political clout needed to wed a prince in a decade or two. Uritz is not so rigid with its nobility as elsewhere. And I do have six brothers. I'd welcome you as a sister-in-law, but I can't wait a decade to marry."

The girl pulled back from his touch and gathered the baby in her lap, so she would not risk him falling from her distraction. "Do you think I could so easily substitute one prince for another, as if which brother didn't matter?!"

Leifhound gave her an assessing look. "You want a crown?"

"Oh, may your father live forever!" she snapped. She wanted to storm off with the baby but settled for snuggling little Michter to her. She kissed the baby's head, so she could blink back tears without Leifhound seeing.

"Are you in love with me, little witch?" he asked as though the idea both intrigued and surprised him.

The girl thought carefully before she answered. Leifhound vexed her, but she was increasingly fond of him despite his faults. "I think...if I saw you every day...I would be."

"I'm flattered."

The girl thought further about how it would be to watch Leifhound marry another woman for political reasons and shuddered. "If you won't even consider me, I should leave Uritz."

"I don't want to chase you off," Leifhound said earnestly.

"Why?" she challenged. "Because you think I'm clever and want to see me every day? Because you want to take care of me?"

Doubt and regret did not sit well on Leifhound's features. He fought them off and replaced them with a cynical smile. "You would make fidelity difficult, wouldn't you?" he sighed. "My future bride deserves that much from me. I don't want you to go, but it's not my desire to be cruel either."

"I can't stay," the girl said sadly.

Leifhound plucked up a blade of grass and broke it slowly into pieces. "Make me two promises before I let you go?"

The girl made no response but gave her attention.

"I know you were born there, but don't give Gourlin the advantage of your talents. Gourlin's king has taken to calling himself an Emperor. It's a fool's errand to invade Uritz, but if they had you, they might manage it or at least become foolhardy enough to make the attempt."

"I don't see how I'd make a difference," the girl said.

There was no laughter left on Leifhound's face. "No one knows how the desert grew, but I suspect your father or someone like him to be behind it. If so, I'm sure you'll be equally impressive with time. I hope you've come to love

Uritz enough to preserve the land of free men."

"I'll swear loyalty to no emperor," the girl vowed. "What's the other promise?"

"Never marry unless you find a man worthy of you."

The girl gave the prince a wry smile. "And how shall I measure that?"

"High or low, he must be man of unerring goodness. Anyone less would take advantage of your talents."

"Like you wanted to do?" she asked.

"Yes," the prince admitted. "Though in my defense, I only planned to use you to preserve my peace and Uritz's freedom. Many others would be less high-minded."

Chapter 25

While the girl packed her things, Leifhound sulked as only a youth can sulk when he realizes a rainbow cannot be kept in a pocket. He tried tempting her with Angsfel, guilting her with Michter, and reasoning with her over Pieter's education, even bribing her with gold, but the girl was resolute. At length the prince did as everyone must when a rainbow fades, accept it and hope for another.

Once again she sold or gave away everything that was not a necessity for travel or too precious to lose and bought a heavier coat. Still her bags were heavy with gold, books, and her new dresses. On Leifhound's suggestion, she decided to travel north as a pegasus.

"You may risk someone trying to capture you," he told her. "But no one will try to shoot you down. It's against the law to wound a pegasus, and they're far more valuable alive."

Against practicality the girl wished the prince would kiss her goodbye, but he found it easier to feign indifference. After she transformed, he did adjust her saddlebags and wish her safe journey.

She had determined to return to Gourlin to reclaim her books, which had weighed on her mind like abandoned children. But she had waited too long to ride back with the flying caravan, who wintered south at the Laughing Peak, so she flew north between the mountains to go the long way around the desert.

While the girl could take on the form of a small pegasus, she found she was not nearly so hardy. As the cold grew more severe, she forgot about Gourlin and looked instead for a place where she might keep warm. After days of searching, she found a small village by a narrow river.

Given the habit of private holds in remote parts of the mountain, the villagers of Bracer's Low found a girl emerging alone from the woods to be unusual but not unthinkable. They were not unkind people, and the coming winter bred solidarity for the fight against the elements. The girl was soon directed to a farm where she was able to find shelter for the brumal season, sharing a room with a farm girl her own age.

The company helped heal her wounded heart.

Verity was a typical farm girl of thirteen. She worked hard, talked a lot, and was a little silly. She was the second of four children. Her older brother was a thick fellow, too interested in pursuing the village milkmaid to pay any attention to their gawky guest. The younger brother and sister still played the games of small children. They loved the stories the girl told them, but otherwise found her too melancholy. The parents were typical of Urite farmers: hardy, practical, and hard-working with easy manners and simple wants. They considered her books and education to be frivolities unfit for a mountain girl, so the girl took care not to reveal her other talents.

Sunny Verity was happy to fill the girl's time. She spoke endlessly of boys and needlework and chickens. She found it curious that the stars had names but only cared that they were pretty. The girl learned all the business of the village from her in far more detail than necessary and with too much speculation to be practical.

At night, they squeezed into the same bed, and Verity liked to snuggle against her captive friend's shoulder for warmth. The girl loved her much the same way she had Michter but found her conversation about as stimulating.

While the family were good and comfortable people, their simplicity of thought and lack of imagination grated on her. She came to understand better that magic was not the only thing which made her unusual. There was no place in Uritz for an educated peasant. She began thinking again about Middlefort, and the city behind the high walls grew more alluring and less intimidating.

When the snows stopped, the girl was eager to be on her way. On the first warm day, she said her goodbyes and hurried as fast as legs and wings could take her out of Uritz. She joined a small band of nomads and traveled with them over the grassy hills north of the Gourlin desert. She eventually found her way back to Paradox without serious misadventure. Her reunion with her books was a happy one for she discovered them unmolested.

She determined not to be parted from them again and spent her gold on a proper caravan wagon, large enough for her to sleep in at night, and an ox to pull it. She traded her heavy fur coat for colorful scarves and simple cloaks more appropriate to the southern climate and warming weather.

She also bought a small, dull mirror, so she could check the consistency of her faces. She was no longer content to be as Leifhound wanted her with a plain face in the most common colors. She was tired of being ignored. So she changed her hair and eyes to the rarest and most vibrant shade shades of red and green. While there is a beauty to any healthy girl or boy, the girl did her best to make her own brand striking. She could accomplish by will what most women could only manage by makeup.

With her new face and wagon, she made a slow and easy journey along the stone road to Middlefort. She picked useful herbs when she spotted them on the roadside and spoiled her ox by letting him graze whenever he pleased. She tied the herbs to the edge of the wagon's wooden roof to let them dry as they rolled along.

Though she stayed in her wagon rather than a tavern, she met other travelers coming and going on the road. Their eyes did not look past her so easily now, though most just bid her a quick hello in passing.

On the second day, the driver of passing a wagon took off his hat to her and slowed his horses. "Hello, there, pretty lady. And what's your name?"

The girl laughed. "I need no name, sir. I am a sorceress."

Chapter 26

The stone walls that surrounded the city of Middlefort at the center of Gourlin were tall and thick, not only for protection but because they channeled water from the river, that had originally run through the city, around it. The channels provided water to a series of fountains both inside and out. To divert more of the river water that flowed in through the northeast, a significant series of irrigation channels supplied the northeastern estates, and a reservoir captured the excess. There was a channel that flowed through and under the city, still following the path of the original river. It had been filled in and built over so much it was barely visible inside the walls but emerged above ground far beyond the walls and stone road to the southwest and carried with it all the things a city needs to have swiftly carried away.

There were ten gates in the city walls to match the ten roads. Four main gates stood facing the cardinal directions; with smaller ones to the northeast, southeast, and so to the west; and two tiny ones, more like doors, in unobtrusive places.

The girl entered the city by the northwest gate and was only vaguely aware of this massive feat of engineering. Her attention was instead drawn to the crowd and soldiers standing guard and a faint awareness that she knew more of the laws of Uritz than her own country. The tight, tall buildings and crowded byways told her that finding a place in Middlefort would not be as simple as claiming a hold, even assuming one could find an empty spot to claim.

While she drew a few glances, in the city, it took more than an ox and a pretty face to stand out.

There had been crowds in Loch High, but it had never felt so crowded. Nor had there been so many carts and wagons. She followed slowly behind the cart that went before her, suddenly unsure of where to go now that she had arrived. The entirety of the city was paved in stone, and the main roads were wide enough for two wagons to pass without difficulty. She stuck to these and attempted to tour the place.

The main roads of Middlefort crisscrossed from gate to gate like a deranged and over zealous pentagram. Either by design or happy accident there was no direct way to go from north to south or east to west The city was cut into triangles occasionally interrupted by a circle or piece of a circle. Most of the gates had something of a courtyard area just inside to avoid clogging. The girl got lost more than once, but she told herself this was normal when one lacked direction.

The city within the walls was large enough to have its own hill and valley, and the most important buildings were up on the hill. After many hours of zigzagging the girl made her way to them. There were a few patches of greenery here, but they were small. The Emperor's private dwelling was one of the few buildings with an actual garden, but it was obscured by courtyard walls, only visible through the iron gate, which stayed locked, barred, and guarded on both sides. It was a very large house, so pale it was almost white, more tall than wide, but modest in scale to the castle where she had spent so much time in Uritz. The Gourlin Emperor displayed his wealth in other ways like gold tipped points

111

on the iron gate. There were full-sized glass windows; in Uritz the castle windows had been mostly lattice work and wooden shutters. The guards were dressed in richer material with higher plumes on their helmets than seemed practical for soldiers. The guards themselves were tall and more attractive than chance alone was likely to cast them. While she was sure they served a practical purpose as well, the girl believed their main one was decoration.

Beside the Emperor's private house and on the very top of the hill was the Forum where laws were made and men debated and argued. The Forum was an enormous building, open to the public, though certain sections were reserved for the lawmakers. Gourlin made no effort to teach its children history, but the girl would come to learn that a counsel of noblemen who advised the king privately had been replaced by a Senate (made up mostly of the same noble families) who preferred open and public debate. In theory, any man could bring a subject to the Senate's attention; in practice, it was a difficult and involved process to be heard. Less ornately dressed guards made regular patrols to dispel troublemakers. They gave the girl friendly but rigid nods when she tried to greet them.

She was told of a place where she might park her wagon and tie the ox for a short time and small fee. This put strain on her pocket, but it seemed a worthwhile expense to walk around for a bit without risk of her things being stolen.

Opposite the Emperor's ornate house on the other side of the Forum was the University where anyone with sufficient money and time could study mathematics, science, law, philosophy, or other obscure subjects with the help of Masters. Wedged beside the University was the Library, and while it was a humbler building than the other three, it was the one that most excited the girl's imagination. Like the Forum, it was open to the public but with no small number of rules. The books and scrolls contained within were not allowed to leave. The University students and Masters were allowed to claim first pick. Lawmakers, their assistants, and other noblemen were to be deferred to politely. So the most popular works were all but inaccessible to peasants.

Copying was allowed but only under the strictest supervision and many found it more practical and less stressful to hire a scribe for this job. The library employed a hundred scribes who worked in rooms on the top floor. However most of their work involved making copies of government documents, so they were very slow to produce fresh copies of books.

Even so, the number of books was a beautiful and overwhelming sight to the girl. Despite the crowds and smells and confusion, she determined to stay in the city.

She started making inquiries, and while she received several offers of shelter, it took quite a while to find an agreeable one that would accommodate the ox and wagon as well. At length she was directed to an older portion of the city where decrepit buildings had been torn down to make way for new ones. Since a city is a poor home for an ox, she sold the animal and used the proceeds to pay the rent on a portion of an empty lot where she could park her wagon.

While the west coast (Uritz included) was rather rigidly Monotheistic, Gourlin (particularly Middlefort) was a babble of religious confusion. Alongside the Monotheist were Atheists, Moralists, Pillarists, Polytheists, a growing cluster of Animists, Panists who tried to believe in everything at once, and defeated Agnostics who found they had too many choices and hoped it would all sort itself out eventually. All of them took a very different stance on their perception of magic: some claiming wizards were godborn holy men who had abandoned them for their sins, many who had muddled magic and witchcraft and did not believe one to be any better than the other, and quite a few more who thought the whole idea was absolute nonsense best regulated to children's stories.

Despite her declaration on the road, the girl decided to take Leifhound's advice and not draw the attention of any of them. She made cures for colds and similar complaints and sold them as many others who claimed to have some medical education would sell bottles of random ingredients which worked more on positive thinking than good science.

As the girl's cures worked with far more consistency and her prices were fair, she found herself with a steady stream of regular clients. Most were not concerned with who she was, but those who asked she deflected by saying she was a student of the Library. And this was reasonably accurate.

While her talents could have made her rich as Leifhound suggested, she only kept her business open enough to pay for her rent and necessities. She devoted as much time as possible to the Library. She still felt she was a novice at her peculiar trade and was determined that, if she was to be the only sorceress in the land, she would be a great one, a true master of the art of magic. She set herself to two main tasks: first, the study of languages so she could unlock the secrets of the books she bought in the Loch High bookstore, and second, the scouring of the Library for forgotten texts on the magical arts.

While it was permissible for all to enter the Library, a pretty young girl in humble dress and no escort drew more than her fair share of attention. Some of this was kind.

Young men with grins were overly helpful and talked too long. The few young women she encountered looked at her with a mix of envy and curiosity and often warmed to her quickly when she was given a chance to speak to them. But their escorts, whether men or women themselves, usually steered them away after a dubious glance in her direction. The scholars and noblemen frustrated her. Even if they had finished with a book themselves, they preferred to tease her rather than hand it over. The taunts varied in tone, some cruel, others kindly, but many of them ran along the lines of the books being too difficult for her or the Library no place for a woman.

If she dared to ask a question or state an opinion, they gave her a long suffering glance like she was the most trying simpleton. It made her miss Leifhound and want to snap back that she had counseled princes, but she suspected this would only make the men laugh more and do Uritz a disservice. The Masters were the worst because she desired to speak with them most of all, to ask questions and join their discussions, but they would only shush her and wave her away.

While she had a growing distaste for the subterfuge, she began to take on the shape of an old man to aid her peace while she studied. She bought appropriate clothing for this visage and made him look as scholarly and unassuming as possible. While most people offered her a quiet respect, they did not bother her. The Masters who shunned her opinion as a girl were quite happy to listen to her as an old man. She found this useful but maddening.

Sometimes she came as herself just because she thought it would do the scholars good to see a young girl doing the work of a scribe or a student.

Her search through the dustiest corners of the Library yielded fruit. She found a book on magical ethics, which began to work as her own religious foundation. She read other books on natural science and anatomy, which are very important for those who wish to use magic responsibly. She found a book of very advanced magic in a very old language, and since there is no lower thief than one who steals from a library, she spent over a year making a careful copy.

She was not as careful with her money as one who wishes to build wealth should be. Her tastes were not extravagant, but she preferred to pay for others to cook her meals and wash and mend her clothes so she could devote more time to her studies. She bought things that caught her fancy and gave what surplus she had to the crippled beggars on the street.

From this class, she took a select few as special clients. She pretended to be a student of medicine and offered them free treatments if they would allow her to try her skills on them. Since many of the men and women in this class of life had little or nothing to lose, most of them accepted her offer. She healed a leg bone that had been shattered and useless, made a bent back straight again, and removed a cosmetic deformity, but she worried she had taken on more than she could handle when she tried to restore sight to a blind man. Eyes were complex and delicate, as easily harmed from over growth as too little of it. The gaunt, middle-aged man returned to her for the warm meal she provided, but the process stretched over several months of frustration.

They did not become friends exactly, but they told each other stories over warm tea, which eased their loneliness. The blind man had spent his youth as a soldier, and she learned enough of war from him to wish to avoid it.

116

All this time, the girl grew a little older, a little wiser, and a good bit taller. She had been in the city two years, before her success with the blind man brought her trouble.

Chapter 27

A man who once limped and now walks straight, or a woman who stopped complaining of her back, had not excited the imaginations of the jaded Middlefort inhabitants. The girl with the deformity had lived her life behind a veil, and no one recognized her when she took it off. But the blind man had been what one might call a respectable beggar, with many men who remembered him from his better days and considered his blindness to be a regrettable but honorable war wound. Had his injury not made him bitter and poor company, he would have been well cared for by friends.

The restoration of sight for the old soldier was another chance to be useful and earn his keep rather than beg for it. It rekindled his self-respect and filled him with a joy that could not be kept to himself quietly. So despite the girl's request for discretion, he ran to share his good fortune with old friends, some of whom were officers in the army. The restored sight of the blind man was not half as remarkable as his restored spirits, and he drew the curiosity and stirred the imagination of many. While at first he was reluctant to reveal the girl's secret, his friends pressed him, and he soon found himself speaking of her, favorably, but openly.

The girl found herself suddenly popular, which is often not as nice in practice as it sounds in theory. The rumors exaggerated her beauty which made it worse. Skeptics, admirers, and new clients flocked to her little wagon in such numbers that she holed up inside it until most of them left.

The officials asked her if she had filed permits that she did not know she needed and wanted her to produce records she didn't keep. One of the city guards took pity on her when she broke down into tears and walked her through the process.

His name was Swarf, and to buy her time to adjust, he arranged for a very official looking sign to hang on the door, saying the business was closed pending proper permits.

While the girl could understand math, she found no joy in it, so Swarf found her a bookkeeper to establish her records and figure her taxes. She had never dreamed buying and selling could be so complicated. The office that issued permits got locked in a debate over whether her healing of a blind man should qualify her as a doctor despite her lack of appropriate schooling, which meant they could not decide which permit to offer her.

Her landlord was generous enough to let her rent slide until they had sorted it out, but the girl regretted not having kept more back from her earnings. The Pillarists or Polytheists...she could not keep them straight...kept leaving her gifts of flowers, which she tried to explain she could not return any favors for until the permit situation was sorted out, but they insisted she could bless them without documentation. Swarf saw to it that she didn't starve and soon made it clear his attentions were not disinterested.

He was not good looking or clever like Leifhound had been, but he spoke respectfully to her and was not offensive to the eyes or other senses. He was patient but made it clear that he wanted to marry her. As he was assigned to the city guard, there was less risk of her dealing with the lonely periods a soldier's wife is often subject, and the stress of her permit situation made the promise of being taken care of sound appealing. Her heart was free, but she was reluctant to let Swarf kiss her.

While the thought of Leifhound no longer pained her, she had not forgotten her promise to the prince. There was enough of a Urite still in her to respect a law, or in this case a promise, because it was wise and practical. She was uncertain if marrying a man who had pledged loyalty to the Emperor of Gourlin was the same as giving that loyalty herself, and as to Swarf's worthiness, she was not clear how to measure her own merit much less his.

So she stalled, which only seemed to increase Swarf's attentions. She tried to continue her studies but found it more and more difficult to concentrate. The people at the Library had changed the way they look at her. Young and old began approaching her with every rumor and question they had ever had concerning magic and witchcraft. Some were quite pleasant conversations, but others were not. And this too soon became tiresome. She was intrigued by a rumor of a witch in Netheriaden that she heard from multiple sources. She wondered if the woman was really a witch or just mislabeled as she had been.

To seek relief, she returned home to reread her book of fairytales. She understood them differently now that she was older and knew more of the world. There were truths and lessons deeply woven into the myths that she came to recognize, even shifters like herself. A story of an old woman who tested a woodcutter in the forest gave her an idea for trying the goodness of Swarf.

She changed herself to look like a bent, withered old woman, put on her rattiest cloak, and went looking for her suitor. She found Swarf walking with his soldier buddies and placed herself in his path. "Can you spare a coin for this hungry soul?" she asked extending a palm out to him.

Swarf knocked her hand away. "Find a way to be useful old woman," he barked. "And don't block the path of guardsmen." His fellows, already a little tipsy, laughed and pushed past her, forcibly knocking her into the wall.

Her disappointment was quickly overshadowed by anger and a sense of outrage. She restored her own face and screamed an insult at him, which stopped all the men in their tracks. She ignored the others and stared directly at Swarf. "Do not come by my wagon again! I can no longer stand the sight of you!"

Had Swarf offered an apology or attempted appeasement, her anger might have cooled. But he was far too disturbed by seeing the girl he had been courting in the old hags clothes. His silence sealed her disgust, and the girl ran back home to fume quietly.

A few days later, she returned to find the side of her wagon had been pelted with rotten fruits and the words "BE GONE WITCH" written on the side in mud. She had sealed her door with magic, but it was clear from the broken handles that entry had been attempted.

As she washed the mess away, she decided she no longer had any desire to wait for permits. She went to some of her old customers and offered them unsold cures they might want. With this she raised enough money to buy a fresh ox and left the city.

Chapter 28

To still her anger as she rode out of the city, the sorceress forced herself to think of every kind man or woman she had ever met. This left her sad but less prone to revenge or murder. She wondered if she had been foolish to leave Uritz but could not muster the desire to return. She hated the feeling of having nowhere to go, so she decided to follow the rumor and find out if this witch of Netheriaden existed.

Her time in the Library had left her more familiar with Gourlin's geography. She knew Netheriaden was a country to the east, between Gourlin and the eastern pass through the High Mountains. It was flanked by two rivers that emptied into Gourlin on the north and south. And like many of Gourlin's neighbors, it paid a tribute to avoid invasion.

It was two days journey down the stone road towards Passin and another two to the outpost that sat on Gourlin's border. The journey gave her time to calm down and think. When she reached Passin, she bought a brush and paints and emblazoned the side of her wagon with the word SORCERESS in large, bold letters the same way traveling showmen often painted MAGICIAN on their wagons.

Since she was in no great hurry, she allowed the ox to set the pace again as long as it stayed on course. She lost her desire to be courted, but in case it returned, she made a list of essential qualities before she would consider a man. Between her own list and Leifhound's request, she figured he would be a rare fellow and most likely unavailable, but she was starting to suspect she might be wasted as a wife after all.

She stopped at the next tavern and performed a show much like she had when first making her way through Uritz, only with a few fresh additions such as keeping several utensils and a plate spinning at once. This was merely a magically enhanced act of balance, but it brought applause and some appreciative coins.

She did the same at Postsix on the edge of Gourlin, and they gave her no trouble, only papers to help prove her nationality when she returned. Not that any of the soldiers were likely to forget the beautiful traveling sorceress with the red hair and quick wit, but it was procedure.

It took weeks of rolling down the dirt roads, stopping at every tavern, pub, and small town to find the information she sought. People took her for a traveling entertainer, and she had learned enough discretion not to announce that she was looking for a witch.

In Neiceden, she heard tell of the witch at Haiden and followed the road, if one could call it a road, in that direction. The bumpy dirt paths that passed for roads in Netheriaden made the going slow and full of potholes. While Haiden was almost directly east of Neiceden along the path of the river, no one had seen fit to make a road connecting the two. Instead she bumped along the dirt road north to Folden before heading south to Haiden.

She might have missed Haiden if the road had not ended there. It was a tiny little village just bigger than a hamlet. There would be no pubs or taverns here, though there was a crude little wooden structure she took to be a townmeet. She tied her ox to a post on the fence before it and tried to decide which of the few curious people eyeing her to approach first. She settled on a man with a brown cap and white mustache, took a deep breath, and prepared herself for another onslaught of the Eastern Mountain tongue.

It was not quite another language but had a bad habit of replacing familiar letters with strange neighbors and distant cousins. Hoping she was near the end of her quest, she decided to try the direct approach. "Hello, sir. I heard a rumor that you had a witch in these parts."

"Aye, we hat a wich. See be dere ouvfyde de tillage," replied the man with a tip of his chin in the right direction. "Whav chu wan wid hy?"

"Just a talk, I think," the young sorceress said. "To see if she is what they say."

"See be dav, buv chu bevf be vfayin' away."

The girl nodded to pretend she understood and untied her ox. She rode in the direction the man had indicated, eager to be in and out of Haiden soon as possible. She soon came to a modest hut of a similar construction to the townmeet. Compared to Gourlin, Netheriaden was a very poor country. Stone construction was rare, and the wood was dark with wear and age. There was nothing particularly ominous about the appearance of this hut, except perhaps a few small animal bones that dangled like a wind chime by twine from the edge of the roof, but the wary sorceress pulled up short. There was something off in the sound of the wind.

A woman in a faded black dress and grey apron looked up at her with strange eyes that were both shiny and hollow. She was a spare woman with wild hair in a messy bun. Her worn face might have been pretty once or could be with greater care. "What chu want?" the woman shouted out to her.

124

Since the woman had left her Ts intact, the young sorceress called back, "Are you from Gourlin?"

"Long go," the woman said. "Didn't like it."

"May I talk to you?"

The woman nodded, tilted her head towards the door, and walked inside carrying a bucket of water. The cautious sorceress took this as an invitation. She hummed a tune of calm to the ox but did not try to tie him down. The creature was already busy grazing. It did not seem to share her apprehension.

The sorceress made her way to the door, trying to get a hold on what troubled her. By the threshold she realized there was no song here. The house was filled with something beyond silence, nothingness, a horrible gaping void. Fear crept into her. She was more frightened than she could ever remember, not even when the old man had died. There had been silence then, a warm body gone still and peaceful, but this... there was no peace here.

"Come in, child," the woman said, taking a seat on a stool by the back wall. "I won't hurt you."

Despite her fear, she stepped inside. "Are you a witch?" she asked.

"Some would call me that," said the woman with a strange smile. "You've come a long way to seek me out."

There was shrill scraping like carpentry nails across a slate board. Though it was not a sound per say, the sorceress covered her ears to ward it off.

"You can hear them too?" the witch asked. "A real magic user, as well as a beauty. The spirits tell me you have been offered a crown."

The sorceress allowed a bitter chuckle. "Your spirits are wrong. It was quite the opposite."

The witch laughed in a different tone. The nails screeched again. "You did not listen closely. He told you how to have him."

Though the words were spoken years ago, the girl remembered them well. "He said a nameless girl with no father will not do. He must marry a woman with political connections."

The witch smiled kindly. "And he also told you that you could be anything you wanted to be, anyone. Use your imagination."

"I can look like anyone," the sorceress admitted. "But that's not the same as being someone."

"If you were to replace a nobleman's daughter, who would know the difference?" the witch asked.

"The daughter for one," the sorceress replied. "I can't just take someone's life away from them."

"Couldn't you?" the witch asked. "If you fail to act, your prince will marry another."

The sorceress did not want to even contemplate what the witch was suggesting. When had locking up the princess to take her place ever worked out for a fairytale enchantress? "My happiness is not worth another's sorrow. Leifhound is free to marry as he pleases. A good heart is won through honesty, not deception."

The witch sniffed, while the scrapping and scraping grew more shrill. "Men's hearts are fickle, but a crown is a prize worthy of certain sacrifices."

"A crown is a heavy burden," the sorceress retorted, ready to turn on her heels. "I wouldn't want it. I'm sorry I came and bothered you. I'll go now."

"Wait!" the witch yelled to halt her. "I have something else you'll want."

Chapter 29

The witch rose from her stool and took a dusty book from the shelf. "I thought I might try my hand at magic years ago, so I acquired this. But I could not work it. The spirits tell me you have something to trade for it."

The sorceress knew what the witch wanted but was reluctant to hand it over. She had kept the book on witchcraft from the shop in Uritz, for she had not had the heart to burn or discard it and thought it too dark and dangerous to sell.

Still the magic book called to her like a prisoner from a dark cell. She went to her wagon, took the other book from where it was buried under others in a chest, and returned with it. They exchanged the books like trading hostages.

The sorceress hurried away with her rescued book, vowing to never again seek out such a person. She drove her wagon on the most direct route out of Netheriaden and back to Gourlin. By the time, many days later, when she reached the border and the smiling soldiers of Postsix with her papers, she had stopped shivering and left her fear behind.

Her solitude now seemed complete, but she understood there were worse things than loneliness. The soldiers flirted with her to earn her smile, and she smiled for them but guarded her heart. Short term friends were better than none.

She grew tired of marketing herself as an entertainer,

and when she rolled her wagon again through Passin decided to add the words "Purveyor of Medicinal Cures" under the word SORCERESS. She returned to her old trade of peddling magical potions. While she knew many would think her no better than the other swindlers with their elixirs, at least she had the comfort that hers would do actual good.

The wagon allowed her to avoid any trouble with permits. She found a way to secure little pots to the wagon roof, so she could grow the herbs not easily found by the roadside. Her talents allowed her to dine with both the highborn and low, but she formed no new friendships. The poor were too uneducated, and the nobility too insufferable to hold her interest. Sometimes she would come across a case which excited her pity, and she stayed in one place for a while to perform a more complicated cure. She toured Gourlin with her ox and wagon, following each of the stone roads to its end and beyond. When she had exhausted every other road, she returned to Ellsworth.

She rolled her ox and wagon straight through the center of town. People gawked, but no one told her that animals were not allowed. She was quite grown now, taller than most men because she wanted to be. Though her clothes were still appropriate to a traveling merchant, she held herself like a noblewoman. This seemed to give people pause.

She had changed so much and so often the bookseller did not recognize her when she entered his shop, but she was glad to find him well. His son was now old enough to help in the bookstore. The sorceress, who still had no name, had come back with the idea of telling the bookseller about her adventures, but seeing the boy sweep the floor under his father's watchful gaze made her hesitant to disrupt their steady lives. She took her time choosing two books and made no attempt to haggle over price. She complimented the workmanship on the binding as she counted her coins out on the counter.

The bookseller swept up her coins with his long fingers, and as she turned to go asked, "Did you find your father?"

With the bright smile of a young girl, she asked, "How did you know me?"

The bookseller glanced out the open window, where her wagon and the word SORCERESS were well visible, even though the paint had started to fade.

"Ah."

So the young sorceress told the bookseller and his son about riding the flying caravan, finding her father's grave, kissing a prince, studying at the great Library, and a few of the other things that had happened to her along the way. While it did the bookseller good to hear, it planted a seed of adventure in the boy's heart, which is sometimes a good thing and sometimes not. But they parted company in good spirits.

The stone road ended at Ellsworth, and the sorceress was tempted to turn back. But beyond her village was another outpost of soldiers that she had yet to visit, and they often proved good customers. Her reunion with the bookseller reminded her of the kind family who owned the tavern, so she decided to visit them at least.

She had been gone too long for them to remember her clearly, but they had remained kind and welcomed her again. She was surprised to learn that their daughter had married recently, at sixteen, to a young man of eighteen from the village, so the sorceress determined if nothing else, she would visit this first friend of her journey.

While it was more often her habit to listen to the world than make up songs, she sang quietly to herself as she rolled down the dirt road.

"I am not the girl you banished,
But are you the town I left?
Will you throw your mud and sticks again
Or lay them down to rest?
Will you recognize me
If I don't change my face?
Am I coming home again,
Or is this just another place?"

The forest was still thick and tall here, so there was no one to hear her. The trees sang the same ancient song, but the road was not so long as the sorceress remembered. She arrived in the village before the sun had set.

Chapter 30

Nettle, for that was the name of the village, had changed little since the girl had been away, but her experience with it had been so limited, it seemed strange to her. It was a quaint little village. The town hall was still painted the same dull yellow from her memory, but it seemed smaller. The scattering of shops were the same that could be found in any small village: a butcher, a blacksmith, a tailor, a carpenter, a tanner. There was an empty space where the farmers came to sell their produce, but they had already packed up and gone for the day. The only new building was a small pub, but as the sorceress had spent so little time in town, she did not realize it was an addition.

She locked the wheels in place and released her ox from his yoke, tying him to a nearby tree with a long rope so the animal might have more range to graze and attend to other ox business. She checked her plants, several of which dangled over the side of the roof, and was ready to spend the night quietly in her wagon, when some young men emerged from the pub and spotted her.

Visitors were not common for such a small village and always excited curiosity. The young men swarmed the wagon like flies scenting honey, but finding the young woman both taller than any of them and beautiful, hovered uncertainly.

"Good evening," the sorceress said and was met by an echo of the same greeting. She had grown easy with soldiers, but these unarmed young men intimidated her. Perhaps cause she knew they were very likely the same schoolmates who had been so cruel all those years ago. "It's late, so I'll open for business tomorrow."

"What sort of business?" one the young men asked.

"Medicines," the sorceress said, climbing back onto the wagon seat for the advantage of height and the small door where she could slip inside. "Cures for aches and pains."

"Do you do any magic tricks?" another asked.

"No," the sorceress said, and because she was an honest and accurate person added, "Not anymore." She graced them with a smile that put the men at ease.

"Let us buy you a drink?" asked a third.

"Or dinner?" offered a fourth.

This seemed a far better welcome than the stones she had feared, so the sorceress nodded her assent. She walked inside the pub and listened to the village gossip as she had in many other places. She refused the many offers of drinks, as a young woman must keep her wits about her in a strange place, and watched as the young men tried to improve their courage by dulling their sense. They asked her many questions.

"Is your husband with you?"

"I have no husband."

"Your father?"

"I lack that too."

"Give us a name?"

"I'm afraid that's impossible."

"Why?" they asked curiously.

With her most disarming smile, she said, "You have yet to give me yours."

After she had been given every name in the pub, she asked, "And which of you charming fellows is not yet married

132

or engaged?" By the time they had finished answering and arguing over that question, they forgot to trouble over her name.

Not long after, she announced a plan to retire to her wagon, and there was a fight over the right to escort her. She ducked out before it was settled.

While not a very vengeful person, she had enjoyed the trouble she caused. She remembered what Leifhound had said about pretty girls and decided to linger for a few days. Besides, she wanted to see a few things before she moved on.

The next morning she found the small cabin on the outskirts of the village where she had lived with the old man. Other people were living there now, so she did not enter. It was no longer home. She returned to find the village awake and several villagers, not just young men, lingering by her wagon. She took her seat and explained her wares but put little effort into selling.

Since the villagers had to send word to Ellsworth to get a doctor, they were willing to try her remedies, even though they handed over their coins with skeptical faces. The gossip came quickly. She did nothing to encourage it but nothing to fight it either. She did excuse herself in the afternoon, so she could seek out her old friend from the tavern. A few quick questions told her the right house. It seemed to ease people's minds to know she had someone to visit.

The young bride remembered her. She was surprised to see the sorceress so changed and flattered the old acquaintance had bothered to seek her out. Having grown up so remotely with only her brothers for playmates, the girl from the tavern thought the village a grand place with plenty of agreeable company. "You're so pretty. I'm sure you'll find a man of your own soon," the young bride said kindly.

"I'm too tall for most men," the sorceress replied, for she did not want to hurt the young bride's feelings with her cynicism.

Since her husband worked long hours, the young wife agreed to meet her friend in town the next day after she had put the house in order. They picked flowers for the old man's grave and walked together to the graveyard. It was this kindness that kept the sorceress from being more elaborate with her little revenges. She had thought about confronting the village about their treatment, and while she never intended to harm anyone, she had considered breaking a few hearts or giving everyone a good scare. But since she had been seen walking with the young bride who was new to the village and enjoyed her married life so well, she did not wish to stir up any trouble which might hurt her friend. Instead she left quietly and continued on to Postnine with its waiting soldiers.

Postnine stood on the southwest edge of Gourlin that looked out upon the desert beyond. She had visited other Posts on the edge of the desert and knew all the soldiers were afraid of it, as though worried it might grow again and swallow them up.

But the sorceress felt no warning of danger or horrible nothingness here like she had with the witch. The desert was quiet and still in a peaceful way, and she began to think it might be the ideal place to attempt her study of more advanced forms of magic. The quiet would make it easier to hear the subtle nuances of magic needed, and the remoteness would take away the likelihood of anyone being harmed if things went awry.

Caravans that dared the desert were few and far between,

but the sorceress questioned soldiers and merchants until she had learned the secrets of desert survival. While the desert stretched long, north to south, a determined caravan with a steady pace could cross east to west in six to eight days.

She practiced by traveling north from Postnine to Posttwelve and then Posteleven, which were numbered by their building date rather than in a consistent placement pattern. There she found a fragile map in the archive that spoke of an old well midway between Paradox and Pinnacle City. It was almost equal distance from Uritz, Gourlin, and Cordance, which she thought she might like to visit some day. This suited her perfectly for even a sorceress needs water, and it left her in service to no single country.

She told the soldiers where she was going, though they did not seem to believe her. She bought a large cauldron for storing water and as much feed and food as her wagon would hold, along with a few other necessities for desert survival, and struck out across the sand to find the well. After three days, she did, but her joy was short lived for the journey proved too much for her ox. The poor creature died less than half a mile from the water.

Through a combination of magic and sweat, she moved the wagon close to the well. The wheels buried themselves in the sand. Over time she cannibalized boards from her wagon and rebuilt it into a hut of crudest construction, kept standing only by the heavy application of magic to reshape the wood. Magic also kept the inside cool, even when the sun was intolerable, and kept her food fresh until she needed it. When the desert had cleaned the bones of her ox, she added them to the construction to ward off the timid and created a sense of mystique for the few visitors she might receive. When she needed something or grew lonely, she turned into a bird and crossed back into Gourlin for a visit. With only a small pack to carry, she could make the trip in less than a day.

As a young girl, she had wondered what had driven the strange old lady to live in the deep, dark forest or the hermit to perch high on the mountain with nothing better to do than wait until a wandering hero crossed their path, but now she understood. They did not hate people. They just needed the quiet and sense of safety, a place to keep things that were special to them or too dangerous to allow a thief to carry off.

There were a few people desperate enough to brave the desert to see her, and when they came she did her best to heal them and send them home. She preferred deliveries of food and supplies to gold and made this as well known as she could. But most of her time was spent in study, alone with her books and the peaceful still of the desert. As the years passed, she grew a little strange but never bitter.

She did not stay forever in the desert. There would come a time, years and years in the future, when another prince would come seeking her aid, and to help him she would travel across the sea to the land of wizards. But that is a story for another time.

For now the woman with no name is content, and you must be too.

The girl's story continues
in the novel *Seventh Night*.

Meanwhile the tale of a desert sorceress
sparks the imagination of a young boy.

The second book in the *Before the Fairytale* set

HORSE FEATHERS
is coming soon...

HORSE FEATHERS
by Iscah

Phillip is a young boy bored by his mundane life on a unicorn ranch. He dreams of adventure and a pegasus, but the most exciting thing in his life are Moralist meetings. That is until his father makes an announcement that will uproot them both and change Phillip's life for ever.

But this adventure is no fairytale. This is the story before the story, a young peasant's view of a storybook world, which teases with wonder through loss and hardship. Phillip must survive by his wits and navigate the lows and highs of society without losing himself.

For News and Updates follow us on

www.amoebaink.com
or
www.facebook.com/BeforetheFairytale

Their stories merge in the exciting adventure...

Once, a boy fell in love with a girl not long before a princess married a charming prince, and if the boy had been the prince or the girl had not been the princess, this might have been a simple fairytale romance.

But he wasn't, and she was. So things were complicated. And then there were the bandits and the poison and the kidnapping and the secrets and the betrayal and the monsters and the magic, the journey across the desert and the journey across the sea, and of course that tax issue.

In a land where unicorns are common place, life can start resembling a storybook. Everyone wants a happily ever after, but sometimes true love requires sacrifices...

Available Now in Hardback and Ebook

www.cafepress.com/AmoebaInk